A
Harlequin
Romance

WELCOME

TO THE WONDERFUL WORLD

of Harlequin Romances!

Interesting, informative and entertaining,
each Harlequin Romance portrays an appealing
love story. Harlequin Romances take you
to faraway places — places with real people
facing real love situations — and
you become part of their story.

As publishers of Harlequin Romances, we're extremely
proud of our books (we've been publishing
them since 1954). We're proud also that Harlequin
Romances are North America's most-read
paperback romances.

Eight new titles are released every month and are
sold at nearly all book-selling stores across
Canada and the United States.

A free catalogue listing all available Harlequin Romances
can be yours by writing to the

HARLEQUIN READER SERVICE,
M.P.O. Box 707, Niagara Falls, N.Y. 14302.
Canadian address: Stratford, Ontario, Canada.

or use order coupon at back of book.

We sincerely hope you enjoy reading
this Harlequin Romance.

Yours truly,

THE PUBLISHERS
    Harlequin Romances

THE
IMPOSSIBLE BOSS

by

JANE CORRIE

Harlequin Books

TORONTO • LONDON • NEW YORK • AMSTERDAM • SYDNEY • WINNIPEG

Original hard cover edition published in 1975
by Mills & Boon Limited

SBN 373-01956-4

Harlequin edition published March 1976

Printed in Canada

CHAPTER ONE

TAMMY DAINTON waved farewell to the Agency truck that had brought her to her destination from Adelaide.

She walked up the immaculate driveway bordered with flowering shrubs, and wished she could have been able to freshen herself up before presenting herself to her employer. The journey had taken just over two hours and it had been hot and sticky in the truck. She glanced down at her linen frock, glad at least that she'd chosen to wear one that didn't crease. She straightened the straw hat on her head and looked ahead of her and stared at the imposing old Colonial homestead facing her. My, it was grand! Well kept too, she thought as she mounted the steps leading to the equally imposing front door. She wondered where the actual farm was. Her employer, she had learnt, was a farmer.

She pulled the bell and waited, gazing back down across the grounds surrounding the homestead. Fenced-off green pastures ran parallel with the drive. They were called paddocks, no different from at home, she thought. In fact, she mused, looking at the well-kept lawns in front of her and numerous shrubs that nestled around the homestead, one could well imagine oneself right in the heart of Surrey, the county she had left only six weeks ago.

Hearing someone approaching, Tammy looked in the direction of the footsteps. The man stopped in his tracks, stared, then came closer. He was at least six foot tall, his blond hair looked almost white from exposure to the sun. As he came closer Tammy saw he was quite bronzed. That was one thing she had to get used to, well tanned beings. Coming from the land of pale faces, as she would have put it, it made a welcome change. Not that there was any welcome in this man's approach, in fact quite the reverse. Tammy would have smiled had there been any sign of softening in his handsome features, but for all the expression they showed they might have been carved out of stone. There was something about his bearing, too, that slightly intimidated Tammy. His blue check shirt and immaculate grey gaberdine trousers suggested boss rather than employee. The type of man who gives orders and expects them to be carried out—or else. Although it was very warm, Tammy shivered. She waited until he came within speaking distance.

'Yes?' it was spoken brusquely as if to say state your business and let me go about mine.

Tammy didn't feel this was a very good beginning. Surely the Agency had let him know she was coming.

'You wanted help' she said. 'I've just arrived.'

The information did not appear to help matters, in fact quite the opposite. She saw his eyes narrow, and noted that they were grey. She wondered what they looked like when he smiled.

'Have you?' he drawled. 'Well, young lady, you can hightail it right back to town.'

Even with the southern drawl the voice managed to somehow sound insulting. 'Aren't you rather young for this sort of thing?' He queried coldly.

Tammy stared at him. She knew she didn't look her age, she ought to have tied her hair back, it helped a bit. 'I'm twenty-two, and I have qualifications,' she replied equally coldly.

His smile was not a pleasant one. 'I'm sure you have,' he drawled, 'but you really should have found out a little more about me, you know. For instance, I prefer taller, and shall we say more curved feminine attractions. I can't say I'm even tempted.'

Tammy was getting a little tired of this uncavalier treatment. What on earth did he mean by tempted? Then her eyes grew larger and she demanded indignantly, 'Do you want help or not?'

He stared back at her, the ice in his eyes even more prominent. 'You're English, aren't you?' She didn't think that worth replying to. As she didn't answer, he carried on. 'I want help—yes—your kind of help, no. If you'll just wait along there,' he indicated the end of the verandah that ran the length of the homestead where there were some cane chairs and loungers, 'I'll see you get transport back to town. Good day to you.'

He walked off and left Tammy blinking in astonishment. Of all the . . . ! She walked to one of the cane chairs and sat down. Her lips straightened. The more she thought about it, the more she was inclined to think she'd had a narrow escape. She wasn't tall enough, and hadn't enough curves. Well! She thought of Maisie, one of the Agency girls, who had wanted this assignment as it was nearer her home, but she had still two weeks to go to complete her present one. Maisie, she felt, would probably have fitted the bill, she had curves to spare. She had saved Maisie from a fate worse than death. She grinned, and wondered whether Maisie would have been grateful, then grew thoughtful again. As soon as she got back to the town, she would get through to the Agency and let them know what had happened. She would get this man struck off the Agency list for a start. She glanced nervously around her, hoping the transport he had promised wouldn't be too long in arriving.

It wasn't. She heard the wheels crunch on the drive before it rounded the bend and a Land-Rover drew up in front of the homestead. Tammy got up and collected her case. The driver, a small wizened man burnt almost black, gave her an odd quizzing look as he opened the car door for her, then placed her case in the back, got back in and started up. He didn't, Tammy noticed, ask any questions. Tammy had an odd feeling he was slightly embarrassed. He kept his eyes on the road ahead, and it was not until they were some way from the homestead that he spoke.

'It never comes off,' he said.

Tammy started and stared at him. 'I beg your pardon?'

He continued to look ahead. 'Rick don't go for no gatecrashers,' he asserted.

'Gatecrashers?' murmured Tammy beginning to feel out of her depth. Then she sighed. 'All right, call me simple, but I haven't the faintest notion of what you're talking about.'

He shot her a look under frowning brows. He nodded his head back indicating the homestead they had just left. 'Rick Hatton, wealthiest landowner this side of the Southern territory. We've kinda got used to this run. There's one thing you girls never take into consideration, and that's that Rick has a mind of his own. When he gets hitched, it'll be in his own time, and with a girl of his choosing, and not with any townie, that's for sure.'

Tammy's eyebrows shot up and she stared at the man. Then started to chuckle as the whole ridiculous situation became clear. The man gave her an uneasy sideways look.

'S-sorry,' she gurgled, 'but I'm just beginning to get the picture. You see,' she managed to get out, 'I c-couldn't understand why I was shot off the place w-without even my qualifications being checked. Oh, dear,' she went on, managing to stop chuckling, 'it's not really funny. It's a long way to come for this kind of treatment.' She straightened her hat. 'Well, one thing is certain,' she said grimly. 'If Mr Rick Hatton still wants a secretary, he can want. I wouldn't take the job if they offered me double pay!'

The man's mouth fell open. He put his foot on the brake, stopped, and turned round to look at Tammy.

'You mean you really had a legitimate reason for coming?' he said, pushing his weathered hat off his brow.

She gave him a pitying look, then relented. It wasn't his fault, after all. 'What's your name?' she asked.

'Danny. Just Danny,' he answered.

'Well, look, Danny, in spite of what everybody seems to think about Mr Hatton's attraction for the opposite sex, he leaves me stone cold. Contrary to your and apparently his misconception, I came, or I thought I came, in answer to an advertisement given to the agency I work for.'

He stared at her. 'Say, you really are a Pommie, aren't you?'

'I should have thought that was obvious,' she replied. 'I've only been in this country six weeks.'

He grinned. 'Well, you know with all those posh accents they're turning out from the big cities these days, it's a bit hard to tell the real thing—mind you, a lot put it on, hoping to impress Rick. Cuts no ice with him, though.'

'I shouldn't think even a diamond cutter would get through that exterior,' she said tartly.

He looked hurt. 'Now just you hold on, young lady, I've known Rick since he cut his first tooth. One of the best, he is. Can't blame a fellow for getting soured on the opposite sex. If you knew what tricks they got up to to wrangle a stay at his place, you wouldn't believe it.' He stared out at the faint outline of hills before them. 'Not to mention his ma running off with a feller and leaving him and his dad when he was a young 'un,' he muttered.

Tammy sighed. So some of it made sense. Still, it was no reason why Rick Hatton should take it out on every female in sight. She said as much to Danny. This produced another of his grins.

'Well,' he drawled, 'I wouldn't say he takes it out on them exactly. He's no monk, if that's what you're thinking. He appreciates a pretty girl as much as the next man, as long as they know their place, that is.' He turned to Tammy again. 'You said an agency sent you? You don't look like a fifty-year-old house-keeper to me.'

Tammy felt she was going mad. 'I should hope not!' she exclaimed indignantly. This produced another grin from her companion.

'Well,' he told her, 'that's what he wants.'

'If,' said Tammy slowly, 'I don't get things straight very soon, I think I shall go raving mad!' She took a letter out of her handbag and looked at it again, then silently handed it to to Danny.

His brows shot up as he read it. 'But you want Jim Hampton's place,' he said. 'It's the other side of town.' He scratched his head under his hat, then with another grin said, 'I can see where the mistake came in. Rick's place is called Wamoshanta, Jim's Wamanta.' He looked back at Tammy. 'See?' he said, as if that explained everything.

'No,' ground out Tammy, who was feeling tired and slightly depressed. 'How do I get to whatever it's called, then?' she asked.

Danny let in the clutch and as the car moved forward said nonchalantly, 'No trouble, I'll take you there.'

Tammy heaved a heartfelt sigh of relief. At last!

Soon they came in sight of the township. It was not as small as the Agency thought it was. Mr Selby had rooted out a map to show Tammy the area she would be working in. He had called the town a 'small place', but she would be able to more or less get herself anything she required during her two months' assignment.

Wooden buildings nudged one another; Tammy caught sight of several stores, and a glimpse of at least one hotel as they drove through the main street. Presently they were on the outskirts of the town, and from here the roads were more in the nature of tracks. Soon they were passing a small pine forest and beyond that Tammy saw the outline of some buildings high up on a distant hill.

'That's it,' said Danny, nodding to where Tammy was staring. 'Good man, Jim, you'll be all right there. Got a daughter, be company for you.'

They entered the homestead grounds and soon came upon several buildings sprawled in spacious comfort around the large paddock they were passing. Tammy caught sight of dairy cattle out to pasture in the distance. This is more like it, she thought; it was still vastly different from the farms at home, here there was so much more space. She heard the clank of cans as they passed one long shed and guessed it was the milking shed. As her eyes roamed over the vast proportions of the farm, she recalled the farms she had often accompanied her father to on his visits during the weekends in an emergency in his capacity as veterinary surgeon.

She felt a brush of sadness; those days had gone, but they had been days of happiness. After her father's death, she had hoped to be allowed to stay on in the same position. His practice was taken over by another vet, and as house and surgery were combined she had hoped to find accommodation in the nearby village and keep her job as secretary and surgery attendant. However, her hopes had been quickly dashed after meeting the new vet's wife. She had been nauseatingly polite, but made it quite clear that they did not intend recruiting any help until they had really settled in. Tammy couldn't imagine her helping her husband in the surgery—not with those delicate tinted nails and well kept hands. She couldn't help wondering rather spitefully how the vet's wife would react to a resectomy. They would have to have help, of course. It was just that they didn't want Tammy.

Jonathan had grinned when she had told him

furiously that she couldn't see why she shouldn't be kept on. 'Look in the mirror, dear,' was his only comment. Her thoughts ran on. Jonathan, the real reason she was here, she shrugged impatiently; she had had a rather trying day without thinking about Jonathan, and getting further depressed.

They turned off from the farm section and went up a small drive eventually coming to the homestead itself. This was a sprawling ranch-type bungalow set in well kept grounds. Lawns and flowering shrubs, borders of gay flowers made it a delightful setting. It wasn't on quite so grand a scale as the Hatton property, but Tammy wasn't complaining.

The screen doors had opened by the time the car drew up in front of them and a large homely-looking man in his fifties came towards them with an anxious expression on his face.

Danny spoke. 'Hi, Jim. Got your secretary here—was some kind of a mix-up, and she landed up at Rick's place.' He threw Tammy a sly grin. 'She kinda got the treatment.'

Tammy threw him an indignant look, then turned her attention to the man who was holding a large horny hand out to her. Relieved that her boss was nothing like her last unfortunate encounter, she placed her hand in his.

'Miss Dainton?' he asked, pumping her hand. 'Gosh, young lady, am I pleased to see you! Rick's housekeeper turned up here, I sent her off not more than half an hour ago. I've been burning up the wires from here to Adelaide, and they told me you'd left. I was beginning to get worried about you.'

Tammy withdrew her hand, feeling as if it had been put through a wringing machine. She couldn't help feeling sorry for the unfortunate housekeeper. She did hope she would turn out to be a formidable women who would make even the masterly Rick Hatton mind his manners.

Still talking, Mr Hampton swept her into the homestead, and as she listened to his almost fatherly concern about her recent misadventure, she rather felt like bursting into tears. It was just tiredness, she thought.

'Mind you, no call to blame Rick,' he went on, ushering her into what appeared to be a lounge. 'Pretty persistent, some of those females, you know. They always manage to sprain an ankle, or run out of juice just outside his station.' He grinned, showing several gold fillings. 'Mind you, I keep telling him it's time he settled down, stop that lark for good and all.' He settled Tammy in a comfortable large cane chair and gave her a quick searching stare. 'Tired, are you? I'll get Paula to show you your room. You have a rest until dinner. Paula will look after you.' He turned and called the name loudly.

A young girl shortly entered the room; her fair hair was pulled back in a pony-tail, she wore jeans and T-shirt. This must be the daughter, Tammy thought. She smiled rather uncertainly at Tammy as the introductions were made.

'Show Miss Dainton her room, Paula, and tell

Esme to get dinner at six—on the dot, mind you,' he ordered, and left the girls together.

'This way,' said Paula shyly.

Tammy followed her through the large airy living room, then through the dining room and down a passage. At the end of the passage Paula stopped and opened a door. 'Here's your room,' she said. 'My room's next door. The bathroom and shower's across there.' She indicated the door opposite.

She followed Tammy as she went into her room. Tammy's case was sitting on the rug beside the bed. The room was homely without being fussy. The bright candlewick bedspread brought the only note of colour into the room, yet it was ample, and the dark highly polished furniture shone with a beauty of its own. It was very old, handed down, Tammy surmised, through the years from father to son. The only new piece was a modern dressing table that looked slightly out of place against the heavy dark red wood.

She turned to find Paula's intent brown eyes fixed on her. She smiled at her. 'It's a lovely room,' she murmured, hoping to put the younger girl at her ease.

'Bit old-fashioned,' said Paula, 'but Dad won't hear of any changes.' She nodded to the dressing table. 'He bought that when he knew you were coming.' She gave Tammy a quick look. 'You're from England, aren't you?' She sat down on the bed and gazed at Tammy earnestly. 'What's it like? Dad came out when he was a boy, but he's always saying he'd like to go back just once.' Her fingers traced the pattern of the bedspread, and she sighed. "I don't think he ever will, he's always getting mixed up in local affairs.'

Tammy sat beside her. 'Well, Paula, it's not much different from here. I mean, there's green belts, and houses and towns.' She stopped and grinned. 'Listen who's talking! I've only been six weeks in the country, and most of that time was spent in Adelaide. Tell you what, you ask me in another six weeks' time and maybe I'll be able to point out the differences.'

Paula grinned back. Tammy noticed how her face lit up, giving her an almost elfin quality.

'Do I have to call you Miss Dainton? We use christian names out here, what's yours?'

Tammy grimaced. 'Tabitha,' she announced with a gleam in her eye, daring Paula to laugh.

Paula cast her a mischievous look. 'Honestly?' she asked.

Tammy nodded gloomily. 'But please call me Tammy, everybody does.'

'Tammy, then,' said Paula, giving her a critical look. 'It suits you,' she said, then glanced at her watch. 'Gracious, I'll be late for dinner, and Dad will be furious, he likes dinner on time.' She rushed to the door. 'Give you ten minutes for your shower,' she called, 'then I bags,' and she was gone.

Hastily unpacking the necessary items for her ablutions, Tammy had the shower and unpacked the rest of her case. She smoothed the linen dress she meant to wear out on the bed. It was lime green, and said to be uncrushable, but Tammy felt she had been had. There were a few pleats where none should be, she sighed, but on further inspection of her other dresses, they were all more or less in the same state. She didn't suppose it would really matter. Mr Hampton and his daughter didn't seem the type to stand on ceremony.

Just as she was brushing her hair, Paula joined her. She too had donned a dress, it was a blue gingham, plain but attractive. Her hair had been combed out of its pony-tail and she looked older than she had at first appeared.

'Ready?' she asked.

Tammy nodded, and the girls went back along the passage to the living room.

Mr Hampton was waiting for them with a tall rangy young man with a thin sensitive face and dark wiry hair. Both men were similarly dressed in khaki drill trousers and white shirts. Mr Hampton introduced the young man. 'My jackaroo, Gerry Teller. Gerry, this is Miss Dainton.' He coughed, 'Er . . .'

Tammy laughed. 'Please make it Tammy,' she said, and glanced at Paula as she did so, wondering whether she was going to let her down, but Paula grinned back at her in a conspiratorial fashion and held her tongue.

Gerry's brown eyes appreciatively acknowledged Tammy as he held out a large hand to her. 'Pleasure, Tammy.'

Dinner was served shortly afterwards by a stout motherly-looking woman with grey plaited hair woven round her head, who gave Tammy a welcoming smile.

This was Esme. Tammy learnt later that she was Dutch, wife of one of the dairymen. Esme acted as housekeeper, cook, and generally saw to the wellbeing of the household. The rough work was carried out by two aboriginal women, liable, she learnt, to disappear from time to time on what was known as walkabout.

The meal consisted of roast lamb, potatoes, and green peas. The servings were enormous to Tammy's way of thinking, but the others had no trouble in demolishing their helpings. The sweet was a jam sponge, beautifully cooked, but even so, Tammy was unable to do full justice to either course.

Mr Hampton urged her to try to finish her sweet. 'You could do with some fattening up,' he told her.

Tammy chuckled and surprised Gerry into a grin. 'Careful, Jim,' he said in a husky voice that Tammy thought rather attractive. 'Young ladies like to watch their figures.'

Smiling, Tammy replied, 'It's not that. I'm afraid I'm what's known as the greyhound variety, nothing I eat makes the slightest difference.' She looked at her employer. 'I'm afraid you've got your work cut out if you want to—er—fatten me up.'

Jim Hampton nodded across at Paula. 'Same thing there. Eats more than I do sometimes, and look at her, takes after her mother.'

Gerry, who had been silent during these exchanges, gave Tammy a shy smile. 'You'll do,' he said.

Paula's eyes opened wide, and she hastily concentrated on her plate.

They had coffee on the verandah where it was cool. Gerry sat next to Tammy and offered her a cigarette. He didn't say much, and Tammy gathered he wasn't much of a talker. She was learning more each day about Australian men.

Mr Hampton questioned her about the Old Country, as he put it, and she was able to bring him up to date with the local politics and the state of the country. They were still talking an hour later when a car turned in the drive. It was quite dark by then and large stars were gleaming in the midnight blue sky. The car door slammed and a voice that Tammy wouldn't forget in a hurry drawled over the intervening space.

'Evening, Jim, any coffee going?'

'Sure, Rick, come on over,' replied Jim Hampton.

Tammy got up and excused herself quickly before the tall figure joined them. 'If you would excuse me, Mr Hampton, I'm awfully tired. It's been a long day. Goodnight, Paula, Gerry.' She walked swiftly towards the screen doors.

'I'd like a word with you, Miss Dainton,' requested Rick Hatton, making it sound more like an order.

Tammy froze and turned round slowly. He had walked over to her, not giving her much chance to avoid the encounter. She stared at him. 'Well?' she asked coldly. His face was partially hidden in shadow, but she sensed he was grinning. He was! She caught the white glint of his teeth.

'Seems,' he drawled slowly, 'I owe you an apology.'

That was all he said. It didn't sound like an apology to Tammy. 'Do you?' she answered in the same cold voice. 'What exactly for?'

She heard the indrawn breath, and could have sworn he made a slight move towards her. However, he straightened.

'I didn't,' he said, and this time the drawl was more pronounced, 'give you what might be termed as a rousing welcome.'

She looked calmly back at him. 'Well, don't worry about it,' she said airily. 'Mr Hampton's since made up for it. I can't help thinking I've been very lucky in my employer.' She turned towards the others, completely ignoring the man standing with clenched fists beside her. 'Goodnight, everyone,' she said, and calmly walked into the homestead.

Fuming as she undressed, she flung off her shoes. Couldn't make it as simple as just a good old-fashioned sorry, could he? Oh, no, Mr High and Mighty Rick Hatton had to make it sound a debatable point. She had a shower, and was brushing her hair when Paula burst in.

'Tammy! Do you know what you've just done? You've just declared war on the big white chief!'

Tammy glanced at her. 'Good,' she said brightly. 'Where do I collect the war-paint?'

Paula giggled, then sobered again. 'No, honestly, Tammy, I don't think you know what you've taken on. Nobody, but nobody, answers Rick back, let alone turns their back on him.'

'Then it's high time they did.' Tammy remarked calmly. 'It does us all good to be taken down a peg or two. That way we don't get too exalted an opinion of ourselves.'

'Tammy!' giggled Paula. 'You sound just like my teacher in Adelaide.'

Tammy grinned and met Paula's eyes in the mirror. 'I only talk that way when I'm good and mad—don't worry, Paula, it doesn't happen often.'

The subject was dropped for the time being and the girls chatted amiably until Paula was ready for bed. Tammy learnt that she was attending college in Adelaide, and was just seventeen. She had bemoaned the fact that she would be away during the week, as it was too far for her to travel daily in to Adelaide, and accommodation had been found for her with a distant relative residing in the city. 'I shall be home at the weekends, though, Tammy,' she informed her. 'I don't really miss much during the week and I'm here for our Saturday dance—there's one tomorrow night. You must come.'

Before Tammy fell asleep she thought about the dance Paula seemed determined to drag her to. 'I might go at that,' she murmured drowsily to herself. Providing a certain 'big white chief' wasn't attending.

CHAPTER TWO

TAMMY woke early the following morning to find the room flooded with sunlight. She lay for a moment or so getting her bearings, then recalled the previous day's events. She could see no problems over her first assignment for the Agency and she was looking forward to actually starting work. Her fortnight spent working at the Agency's headquarters in Adelaide had prepared her for the sort of work she would be called upon to do on the various assignments she would be given, be it outback station, farm, or just ordinary plain business premises. The agencies were not short of work, the problem was staff to cope with the flood of work that they were asked to cater for. Tammy had been given the choice of three, and had chosen the farm on the outskirts of the famous Barossa Valley, seventy-five miles from Adelaide. 'And I'm going to love it, I just know I am,' she murmured.

Her thoughts turned back to home. It was February, the second, to be precise. She wondered if it was snowing, and for one tiny second she felt a stab of heartache. She quickly dismissed these thoughts, and thought about Jonathan. She was still a little peeved over the incident at the airport. He had agreed to her getting away for a while and finding her own feet since her world had been rocked by the sudden death of her father. It had been Jonathan who had seen to everything, his shoulder she had cried on, and his home she had been taken to to recover slowly.

Jonathan had taken up residence with his mother in the village only three years before. They had bought the old manor once belonging to the squire, now deceased. He had made the acquaintance of Tammy shortly afterwards by taking a labrador pup for an inoculation, and began a determined pursuit of her from then on. Tammy, being a modest girl, had been somewhat taken back, he was good looking, wealthy and amusing to be with and could have had his choice of a number of hopeful girls. It did not occur to her to take a good look at herself in the mirror and see herself as others saw her. Her long blue-black hair framing her heart-shaped face, and her wide lovely pansy blue eyes fringed by long dark lashes, might have given her the answer.

Jonathan made an immediate hit with her father and became a frequent visitor at her home. Tammy ought to have fallen in love with him, but she didn't. It wasn't long before she found herself in an awkward dilemma. The whole village expected them to marry, and so did his mother. Jonathan thought it was only a question of time, and was confident he would wear her down in time. On the surface he was gay and amusing, but Tammy had come to recognise the quiet determination that lay under the façade. Owner of an extremely successful wine export and importing

24

business, he was nobody's fool. Now she had lost her father she was completely alone in the world, having lost her mother when she was still a toddler; she had no real memories of her, her father had been all in all to her and they had been very close.

At first she had been so numb she had just let Jonathan take over, but as she had slowly risen out of the cocoon stage, she began to realise how much of her life he had taken over. Little chains were being woven about her. Soon she knew she had to either break free or succumb to the gentle but relentless pressure being placed on her. She had broken free. At least, frowned Tammy, she had made the attempt. She had thought that Jonathan had taken it exceptionally well; there was nothing really he could do about it, she was of age and could please herself.

She recalled her feelings on the plane coming out, of sheer relief. He had understood. He wasn't hurt. All would be well, but when she'd spotted an employee of his on the plane trying to look as if he weren't there, she began to see a little daylight. Jonathan intended to keep watch over her even on the other side of the world. Her destination was Sydney. After arrival, she booked in at the hotel Jonathan had recommended, had tea, freshened up, and booked out again. Jonathan, she knew, had connections in Sydney. It would be no easy task, she mused as she watched the porter place her cases in the taxi, to find a major city he hadn't connections in. The wine importing and exporting business had far-reaching tentacles.

After giving the matter some thought she plumped for Adelaide. Jonathan also knew she intended taking up work eventually and had suggested giving her some introductions to friends of his. Tammy had tactfully refused, pointing out to him that the whole idea of her going was to stand on her own two feet. He had given her a sardonic look and murmured, 'When you've had enough, send for me, I'll be waiting.' And that, thought Tammy was the whole problem, he hadn't taken her no for an answer.

She had an astute guess as to why he hadn't put up much resistance to her going away. Tammy was a home-loving soul. She had loved the village life and had been perfectly content to go on in the same old vein had her life not been suddenly disrupted. Loneliness would be a new and rather daunting experience for her. She had faced this fact squarely, but was certain she would soon make friends. She had had no clear idea what sort of a job she would get. A trained secretary, she knew she would have no problem in getting employment, but the thought of working in an ordinary office appalled her. She had been spoilt, of course. Working for a veterinary surgeon was anything but ordinary; she would not, for instance, be likely to find herself closeted in the office with a basket of kittens, one of which seemed intent on committing suicide by wandering towards a groggy but nevertheless vicious terrier recovering from an operation. Neither would she find herself competing with a parrot

26

while shouting instructions down the phone to a worried owner of a puppy who had swallowed a rubber bone, in desperation she had had to ask the distraught owner to hold on while she searched for a cover to place over the wretched bird's cage perched on the edge of her desk; it was either that or give the phone to the parrot and be done with it!

The thought had occurred to her to seek similar work, but Tammy felt it would bring back too many painful memories. Later perhaps, but now she needed to get right out of her old environment. Her problem was solved when someone handed her a paper on the plane. Idly looking through the advertisement columns, she spotted the Agency's advertisement. They required trained office help willing to travel and work for specific periods as temporary secretaries. Tammy smiled. It was ideal. Not only would she see the country, she would also be out of Jonathan's kindly but over-possessive reach.

A knock on the door brought Tammy out of her reverie. She answered, and a small slight Aboriginal girl sedately dressed in a pink overall entered with a tray of tea.

Tammy thanked her and enquired her name. This produced a giggle and 'Mary, Missy,' then overcome by shyness the girl rushed out of the room.

Sipping her tea, Tammy glanced at her watch. It was seven o'clock. She knew breakfast was at eight and thought she would have ample time to get dressed and wander round the grounds before the meal. She had forgotten Paula whom she met coming out of the shower.

'Hi,' Paula greeted her. 'Like to come to tennis this morning?' she asked.

Tammy regretfully turned the invitation down. Mr Hampton would have plans for her, she was sure, apart from showing her the office routine.

'Well then,' went on Paula, 'you'll come to the dance tonight, won't you?'

'I might,' mused Tammy, then asked as a thought struck her, 'Will he be there?'

Paula giggled, knowing full well who Tammy was referring to. 'We couldn't have a dance without him,' she explained. 'Half the female population in the township would be disappointed if he didn't turn up.'

'Then the answer is no,' Tammy said with finality.

Paula laughed delightedly and pointed an accusing finger at Tammy. 'You're scared of him!' she said.

'I am not,' replied Tammy indignantly.

'Prove it, then, and come,' challenged Paula.

'I don't know anybody,' said Tammy slowly. 'I'm not a one for do's, you know.'

'You know me and Gerry,' laughed Paula. 'Gerry's going to be awfully disappointed if you don't come,' she said slyly.

Tammy looked startled. 'Gerry?'

'He said you'll do, didn't he?'

'Well?' queried Tammy.

'When,' Paula explained patiently, 'Gerry says that, he means you'll do for him.'

'Paula, you're joking! Aren't you?' pleaded Tammy.

Grinning, Paula replied, 'You could do a lot worse, his people have got a big ranch out in Queensland.'

'Hold on!' exclaimed Tammy, slightly alarmed. 'I've only been here five minutes and you're marrying me off already. I'm your father's secretary, remember?'

Paula was plainly enjoying herself. 'Oh, that,' she shrugged.

Later that day Tammy found her resolution not to attend the dance meeting stiff opposition. The whole homestead appeared to gang up on her, even Mr Hampton. 'We don't get much in the way of festivities here Tammy, these dances are only held in the quiet season, so you might as well enjoy them while they last.' Tammy knew she was going to the dance whether she liked it or not.

She had spent an interesting day divided between the office-cum-study and wandering about the grounds. Her first opinion of her new boss had not been misplaced. She found herself warming to this bluff, outspoken but kindly man. As she watched him taking out files and explaining the office procedure, she wondered how long ago he had lost his wife. She had the feeling it was perhaps when Paula was a baby. There were no outward signs of real feminine interest in the homestead—furniture arrangement, decorations such as there were, all appeared to be more for comfort's sake than for impression.

'Anything you're not sure of, just ask,' he told her.

'If I'm not around, make a note of it and see me at dinner—and now young lady,' he said, firmly closing the filing cabinet, 'it's Saturday. I'm not going to ask you to do anything else but enjoy yourself. We'll start the paper work on Monday.' He gave her a crinkled grin that lit up his face.

Tammy wandered over the farm. She wondered how many acres it occupied. Moving away from the buildings, she saw fields of maize and some of wheat, the golden yellow plainly visible from afar. Of the cattle grazing she realised with a spurt of pleasure they were Jerseys and Friesians. She breathed in the soft air and let her gaze pass beyond the fields of cattle. Splashes of pink and white met her gaze and she knew they were orchards. Farther down the valley she thought of the acres of vines they had passed on the way up. What was it that Len the Agency truck driver had uttered every now and again as they had passed a particularly fertile section? She frowned in concentration, then it came to her. He'd said, 'It's beaut.' She sighed in deep contentment, he was right, it was beaut.

After ascertaining from Paula what she ought to wear for the dance and getting out a dress that did not look too plain, she sat in front of her dressing table mirror and debated on what to do with her hair. It was naturally curly, and she had already decided to sweep it back for office duties, but would have preferred to let it hang loose as it felt more comfortable that way. She sighed and started to sweep it back again from her face. Paula came in just as she was clipping it back.

'Tammy' she exclaimed. 'It's much nicer down, why do you want to scrape it back? I wouldn't do that to mine if it was as curly as yours.'

Taking the pins out, Tammy let it fall back and grinned at Paula in the mirror. 'It's more comfortable this way too,' she said, then looked at Paula's dress. It was a light cotton one of pale blue, white stitching edged the square-shaped neck, and round the hem of the dress. Paula blushed with pleasure when Tammy complimented her on her choice.

'You don't,' she answered saucily, 'look so dowdy yourself,' as she eyed Tammy's deep orange silk dress. It had a mandarin collar and gave Tammy an oriental look. 'You should always wear that colour, Tammy, it suits you,' she said, her brown eyes candidly approving.

The girls were collected by friends of Paula at eight o'clock and bundled into the back of a big Chevrolet. The journey took about twenty minutes. The hall was full by the time they arrived. Tammy had some kind of a notion it would be a sort of square dance effort, and was surprised to find a band in attendance and not a couple of fiddlers and piano player. Spotting Gerry, she grinned, a little relieved that there was one male present she could rely on to dance with. To all appearances there was no difference from an ordinary dance at home, except for two facts, one being that the men stayed strictly to themselves on one side of the hall, the second that they appeared to be much taller and broader and all deeply tanned.

As she glanced at them her eyes lighted on the tall figure of Rick Hatton and she stiffened. He stood out in a crowd with that blond colouring of his. He had a small clutch of men around him listening with great attention to whatever theme he was expounding on. Tammy wrinkled her nose; that was one gentleman she devoutly hoped she would not encounter that evening.

The band started up, but no one took the floor. Tammy thought this rather odd. There were several couples obviously ready to dance, but something was holding them back. She glanced at Paula.

'Rick always takes the floor first,' she explained, 'It's a courtesy, as he more or less owns the town.' Then her eyes grew wide as she stared in front of her. Tammy followed her glance. Rick Hatton was striding towards them in a purposeful manner. Tammy's chin went up and she looked right through him. Undeterred, he kept on coming. Tammy was sure he was going to ask Paula to dance and stared up almost unbelievingly at him as he stood before her and held out his hand.

'Miss Dainton,' he said. Tammy was on the point of hastily thinking up some excuse when he caught her hand and pulled her forcefully to her feet and keeping a tight hold on her propelled her to the dance floor. With clenched teeth he informed her, 'I'm afraid you have no choice.'

Tammy was thunderstruck. Rick whirled her into

the dance, his arm was clamped round her waist like a band of steel. Other couples started to dance. He didn't say another word. When the dance was over, he led her back to her seat and left her.

Paula stared after him. 'Well!' she exclaimed. 'I knew you'd upset him, I told you so, didn't I?'

Tammy looked at her, one eyebrow raised. 'Why did he ask me to dance?' she asked, slightly puzzled.

Paula was still working out the implications. 'That's ruined Gerry's chance tonight,' she said. 'It's a bit odd, though, Rick bringing you back here I mean. Usually he takes them to what we call the top table,' she nodded towards a partitioned-off section at the end of the hall where tables and chairs had been set. 'It's for the town dignitaries.'

'Well, I'm thankful for that at least,' retorted Tammy. 'What did you mean by him spoiling Gerry's chances?' she asked.

'Rick not only starts the dance off but chooses his girl for the evening, and like I said he takes them to join him,' Paula explained.

'I'm not his girl or ever likely to be!' Tammy retorted indignantly.

'Well, you're his girl tonight,' said Paula. 'It's the rules. Gerry can't break them. You've been booked for the evening.'

Tammy didn't think she liked the way they ran things around this township. When the band struck up again, she looked round to locate the cloakroom. If she saw Rick coming she would make a dive in that

33

direction. But she didn't have to bother. When she glanced back at the dance floor he had already chosen a partner for that dance.

Paula stared and for the second time muttered, 'Well!' Tammy waited to be enlightened. 'He's never done such a thing before, he must be furious,' Paula exclaimed.

Once again the position had to be outlined to her, and this time it was Tammy's turn to be furious. 'In other words Paula, he's insulted me publicly,' she said slowly.

Paula's eyes were wide and she nodded, then said hastily, 'Don't worry, Tammy, Rick's a law unto himself. I don't suppose many people will notice.'

Won't they? thought Tammy. She glanced around and surprised a few people giving her curious glances. No, she thought, clenching her teeth, they won't notice. Not much! This then was his reply to her cool reception of his dubious apology. What was she expected to do? Go down on one knee and thank him? When she recalled his actual words on that first meeting she got madder. Even if she had been a gatecrasher, as Danny had put it, there was no need for Rick to get so personal. Tammy was a fair-minded person. Had his apology been anything like sincere she would have willingly have accepted it. She was not a person to hold a grudge. But she had sensed the arrogance behind his 'It seems I owe you an apology', and had acted accordingly. For one moment earlier on, she had wondered whether asking her to dance was another way of trying to say he was sorry. Her lips straightened. Instead he had handed her another insult—in front of the townsfolk at that.

'Paula, is there any chance of getting a lift back to the farm?' she asked.

Paula stared at her. 'You can's, Tammy. Rick might just have decided to have this dance with someone else and come back for you afterwards.'

'Oh, no, he won't,' said Tammy. 'He did that deliberately, and I'm not hanging around to be insulted again.'

Paula looked worried. 'We can't ask the Wilsons to take us back, Tammy, not till the dance is over,' she almost wailed.

A partner turned up then for Paula and off she went, leaving Tammy feeling lost. A few minutes later Gerry joined her. His eyes were smouldering, and Tammy could guess the reason. So much for people not noticing, thought Tammy; Gerry had noticed.

'I guess he's a little spoilt,' he murmured.

Tammy smiled at him. 'Gerry, could you take me back?' she asked.

He looked at her, then nodded. 'Sure thing,' he said, and stood up. 'If you'll give me a few moments I'll make alternative travelling arrangements for a couple of lads I brought in.'

When Paula came back Tammy explained what was happening. Paula wasn't too happy about it.

'It might mean a bust-up between the two men,' she said.

Tammy smiled. 'Really, Paula, Rick's made his point. I could sink through the floor and he wouldn't notice.'

However, she was shortly proved wrong. As Gerry escorted her to the outside door, the tall figure of Rick Hatton blocked their way.

'Going somewhere, Miss Dainton?' he drawled.

'Yes,' replied Tammy, meeting the bland gaze with sparks in her eyes. 'Gerry has kindly offered to take me back. I've got a headache.'

He then turned his attention to Gerry, who met his gaze defiantly. 'I think the privilege is mine, you know, Gerry,' he drawled softly.

Tammy sensed the tense situation that had arisen between the two men. Paula had been right.

'For heaven's sake, I just want to go back to the farm,' she said crossly. 'What's all the fuss about?'

Rick Hatton calmly took her arm. 'Then you shall go back,' he said, and led her out of the hall.

Tammy stole a glance at her companion as they left the township; he had not uttered another word since saying she would go back. His profile seemed carved out of ivory as he concentrated on the road ahead. Soon the homestead was in sight. As Rick pulled up in front of it, Tammy fumbled with the catch to let herself out, but it appeared to be jammed. He calmly reached over her and unlocked it. Tammy jumped out quickly.

'Thank you for the lift, Mr Hatton,' she said coldly. 'There's no need to escort me any further,' and she all

36

but ran up the steps to the screen doors. She didn't think it possible for a man of his size to move as fast as he did, but he was before her as she reached out to push the door open.

She stared up at him. Now what? she thought crossly.

'There's another privilege owing, Miss Dainton,' he said softly.

Tammy started. She could guess what it was. But why in heaven's name was he bothering? Suddenly the man in front of her appeared to be ten feet tall, and for the first time in her life Tammy felt utterly defenceless.

'Shall we forget it, Mr Hatton?' she said crisply, trying to still the panic waves pounding in her chest.

'But it's the best part of the evening, Miss Dainton,' purred her tormentor. He was smiling, as if he sensed her fear of him.

Tammy closed her eyes. 'Get it over with, then,' she snapped, and put her face up for the kiss.

He laughed and pulled her to him with a force that knocked the breath out of her. She had been kissed before, Jonathan's kisses that were wild and forceful— at least she used to think they were, they had nothing on the kiss she was being given by Rick Hatton. He absolutely pounded her. When he did let her go, her lips were stinging from his bruising treatment, and her senses reeling. He released her abruptly, so abruptly she nearly fell against the door. She was gasping for breath and felt she had come into contact with a tornado. With wide eyes she stared at Rick.

'Next time,' he said quietly but with a hint of suppressed fury, 'I shall expect a little more respect from you. No woman turns her back on me. Understand? This is my territory; if you want a fight you can have it, but you'll lose hands down. I have a liking for my own way, which you'll very soon find out. Now go and cry on your pillow.' He opened the door and all but pushed Tammy through it.

Tammy's legs felt weak. She prayed Mr Hampton wouldn't stop her and enquire why she was back early. She didn't stop until she had reached her room. Once there, she collapsed on her bed and sat staring straight ahead. She was trembling all over. She couldn't ever remember feeling so emotionally and physically drained. Of all the big bullies! What on earth had he done to her? Kissed her, yes—but something else had entered into it. She shook her head bewilderedly. Whatever it was, she was too tired to work it out. She felt the hot tears sting her eyes, and angrily shook them away. She would not cry. The very fact that he had told her to was enough to stem the tears. She got up wearily and made her way to the shower.

She was asleep by the time Paula arrived back, and was thankfully saved the necessity of explaining the result of the evening.

CHAPTER THREE

TAMMY settled in during the following week. Mr Hampton explained the business of dairy farming.

'We're lucky, Tammy, we're reasonably near the town, so in the milk zone, and we supply the local population with milk as well as cream to the butter factory. Part of the produce goes to the cheese factory, nothing is wasted.'

The actual size of the farm made Tammy's eyebrows rise. Two thousand five hundred seemed a lot of acreage to her, but Mr Hampton informed her that by Australian standards it was considered small.

She found the work to be interesting and varied, and found to her delight that she was not going to be chained to a desk all day. Certain parts of her duties consisted of walking down to the dairy and collecting the daily returns. In this way she met Esme's husband, Fritz. As his name implied, Fritz was German, a small spruce man with twinkling blue eyes. He came to Australia originally, he informed Tammy, to seek land hoping to start a winery, but found the prices too high, and not enough capital behind him. He still had hopes of saving enough to make his dream come true.

As Tammy wandered back to the homestead, she wondered whether he ever would. He appeared quite content where he was, but one had to have dreams. Rounding the drive, she saw the large car parked outside the homestead. She frowned; it was quite impressive. As she got closer she saw it was a Jaguar. She stiffened, sure now; it was Rick Hatton's. As she passed the car she noted the soft leather of the upholstery and remembered the night of the dance and her ride back in the car. Entering the homestead, she heard the voices as she walked down the hall, and knew they were in the office. She stood still for a moment, then changed direction smartly, deciding to keep out of the way until Rick Hatton had finished his business with Mr Hampton.

She glanced at her watch. It was coffee time, so she sought out Esme in the kitchen. Esme was up to her wrists in flour making scones.

'Shall I make the coffee?' Tammy enquired, glad of an excuse to keep her out of the office.

Esme beamed her approval. 'Mr Hatton's come, so put another cup on the tray,' she said.

Tammy hadn't thought of this. She had hoped Esme would take the tray in to them, but after offering her help she couldn't very well refuse. 'Will do,' she answered, trying to sound cheerful about it. She dawdled as long as she dared over making the coffee, hoping against hope that Rick Hatton had taken himself off, but when she eventually carried the tray from the kitchen to the office the drawling voice answering a question of Mr Hampton's met her as she opened the door.

After one quick glance, she did not look at him again. The office was reasonably sized, but even so, the large frame of Rick Hatton diminished it. Feeling his eyes on her, she laid the tray down. 'Thank you, Tammy,' beamed Mr Hampton. She poured the coffee out, noting Rick Hatton had not even acknowledged her presence. Well, it suited her. She had an awkward moment when she realised she did not know whether he took white or black, and was forced to ask. His reply was terse—no thank you either, noticed Tammy, her lips thinning. She handed Mr Hampton his, and placed Rick Hatton's on the desk beside him, avoiding as much contact as possible. Then she turned to go, but Mr Hampton forestalled her.

'Rick's brought some work for you,' he said, and pointed towards the desk. Tammy looked and saw a pile of brown envelopes neatly stacked beside the typewriter. Her eyes sparkled. Just who was she working for anyway? Her reaction did not go unnoticed by Rick Hatton and his eyes narrowed. The sparks made Tammy's eyes appear sapphire blue and they clashed with the ice cold grey ones.

'His book-keeper's sick,' murmured Mr Hampton, uncomfortably aware of the sudden tension in the room. Tammy bit her lip. It wasn't Mr Hampton's fault, after all.

'Very well,' she replied. 'When do you require them?' she asked coldly.

Rick did not reply for a second or so, and when he did, it was in a soft voice that to Tammy's way of thinking was somewhat menacing. 'Would it strain your capabilities too much if I asked for them at four o'clock?'

'Hold on, Rick' exclaimed Mr Hampton. 'There's at least fifty of those dockets, couldn't I send them back with Danny tomorrow morning—you won't want them until then, will you?'

Utterly ignoring Mr Hampton's protest, Rick Hatton continued to watch Tammy steadily. 'Well?' he said coldly. 'You did say you had qualifications, didn't you? I presume you do type with some adequate speed using all your fingers. My book-keeper uses only two, even so, he can clear them under an hour and a half.'

Tammy bristled, and Mr Hampton expostulated, 'Rick!'

She answered in a low voice, striving hard to keep her temper in check. 'Yes, Mr Hatton, I do use all my fingers—we're trained that way, you know,' and saw with some satisfaction his fists clench. 'However,' she continued icily, 'as I have no idea just what is required I can hardly set a time limit to the work.'

'That's fair enough, Rick,' burst in Mr Hampton. 'Jack Tingston knows the work by heart, the names too.' He turned to Tammy. 'They're for the shearing gangs,' he explained. 'Each man has to have a docket, you just need the name and lines underneath for sheep sheared and time taken.' He picked up a list from the desk and handed it to her. 'All the information's here.'

Tammy looked at it. 'I can have these done by four o'clock, Mr Hatton,' she said smoothly, still perusing the list and not looking up at him.

His 'Thank you,' was more sarcastic than grateful.

On the excuse of collecting her coffee, she left the office. On the way to the kitchen she found to her fury that she was actually trembling.

Danny turned up at four o'clock sharp to collect the dockets, primed no doubt to arrive on the dot, Tammy thought sourly. He was cheerful and chatty. How was she getting on with her boss? Hadn't he said he was fair dinkum? Tammy fervently agreed with him. She hated to think that she might have been assigned to the Rick Hattons of this world.

Tammy did not see Rick Hatton for the rest of the week, but she was made well aware of his existence. More work was sent down to her with cryptic notes in his bold hand stating the precise time he expected the work to be ready to be collected. She found herself somewhat bewildered. Mr Hampton seemed to have no objection, as his own work was hanging fire, and Tammy got more incensed. She mentioned that she couldn't let him have the fuull summary of the milk returns for that day, and Mr Hampton just smiled. 'Don't worry, Tammy, they keep a record in the dairy as well. It can wait until tomorrow.'

After he had left, she sighed. She had heard all about the Australian 'mateship', but felt this was rather overdoing things. Why couldn't the wretched man get his own replacement? Then she sighed again. She

43

knew the answer, of course. It was a way of getting at her. Why should he get a replacement when he could annoy her?

As the days went by she learnt more about Rick Hatton's affairs. He was what was known as a grazier. Sheep was his business. Wamoshanta was a station. She tried hard to carry out the work efficiently, for her own pride's sake rather than a wish to please, but mistakes were inevitable, particularly with the rigid time limit schedule placed on it. On one occasion she had not been able to decipher the book-keeper's writing on some orders for equipment required. Mr Hampton's help was not available as he was out on farm rounds, so she had no option but to try to guess the scrawled address, she hoped it was right, but thought crossly that it wouldn't hurt Rick Hatton to correct it himself before posting. Danny appeared first thing the next morning with the said envelope, plus note. Tammy's cheeks grew hot as she read the blunt message. 'There is such a thing as a directory, use it!' She felt like screaming.

During these trying times, Gerry was a source of consolation. He would call in now and again, not that he said much, but Tammy was grateful for the little attentions and rather dry sense of humour that helped her get things back in perspective when her patience had been sorely tried. However, in spite of all these kindnesses, by the end of the week Tammy's nerves were decidedly the worse for wear, and she devoutly hoped Rick Hatton's book-keeper had sufficiently recovered to resume his duties the following week.

Paula came home at the weekend full of news of a picnic to be held on the Sunday at Wamoshanta. 'Well, it's more in the line of a barbecue,' she said. 'The whole town's invited. I must say when Rick throws a party, he throws a party!' she grinned.

Tammy said nothing. Here's one person that's going to be very busy over the weekend, she promised herself.

On Saturday morning Paula brought up the subject of the dance again. 'Coming, Tammy?' she asked hopefully.

'No, thank you,' said Tammy hastily. 'I've got a lot of letters to catch up with.'

'Poor Gerry,' sighed Paula with a glint in her eye.

Tammy looked at her. 'Well, poor Gerry didn't get much of a look in last time, did he?' she murmured sardonically.

'Oh, phooey, that was only because Rick was mad at you. He never stays mad for long. I bet he's forgotten all about it. Be a sport, everyone will think it odd if you don't come.'

'They can think what they like,' said Tammy, 'but I'm not going to that dance and that's final.' As for Rick Hatton having forgotten all about it, Tammy could have enlightened Paula on this fact, but decided to hold her tongue, and she wasn't risking a dose of last week's treatment.

Tammy wrote her letters. She had told the truth

when she had said she was behind with her mail. She hadn't really had time to write before, so much had happened in the short space of time since she had arrived. She debated whether to let Jonathan know her address, but decided against it. You never knew with him, he was just as likely to take it into his head to pay her a flying visit.

She had not long retired when Paula came back from the dance and demanded to know if she was awake. Tammy, who was about to doze off, roused herself and blinked at Paula. 'Can't it wait till morning?' she yawned.

'You've upset Rick again,' accused Paula. 'I said you ought to come to the dance, everybody was asking after you.'

Tammy blinked and tried to make some sense of what Paula was saying. 'For goodness' sake, Paula,' she said sleepily, 'if I don't feel like going to a dance, I don't go. Be a dear and let me go to sleep, tell me all about it in the morning.'

'I just thought I'd warn you, that's all,' said Paula. 'Rick came up to me and asked right out where you were. He also noticed Gerry wasn't there either, and he didn't like that one bit. He left early and was mad as a hatter.'

Tammy just smiled and snuggled down again. She was asleep before Paula left the room.

Paula sighed. Tammy just didn't understand the kind of etiquette extended to a big white chief.

At breakfast next morning Tammy was treated to

a lecture from Paula on this subject. Mr Hampton grinned, but Gerry frowned.

'I don't see what all the fuss is about,' he said in his husky voice. 'Supposing Tammy was sick, she couldn't have gone anyway.'

Mr Hampton joined in the discussion. 'You see, Tammy, these affairs are a sort of get-together. Rick likes to feel we're all one big happy family. His father started these dances years ago, and he keeps up the tradition. The same goes about this barbecue today. If someone doesn't turn up, and they haven't a legitimate excuse he sort of takes it as an insult. Nothing personal, you understand. Don't worry, I expect when he thinks about it, he'll understand, he'll realise you can't be expected to know our ways straight off. If you explain that you had some mail to catch up on he'll be okay about it.'

Tammy drank her coffee slowly. The point about 'one big happy family' struck her as slightly hysterical. She frowned. Was she to blame? It was true she didn't know their ways. Was it really possible to make peace with Rick Hatton? It would hurt her pride, but perhaps she could try. He had said he hoped she would show him more respect, was that what was annoying him? On each occasion she had stood up to him and refused to be brow beaten. She sighed and put her cup down. It wasn't going to be easy for her; she would have to learn to douse her independent spirit. Australia was a man's country, and when in Rome ... She looked up to find Gerry watching her, and smiled at him. 'Why didn't you go to the dance, Gerry?' she asked. 'I trust you had a legitimate excuse?'

Gerry grinned. 'No point,' he said quietly.

Tammy blushed, then to cover her confusion she said brightly, 'Well, as you and I are in the doghouse I suggest we face the firing squad together. Will you hold my hand?'

'Pleasure, ma'am,' he answered solemnly, his eyes twinkling.

At three o'clock Mr Hampton, Paula and Tammy escorted by Gerry set off for Wamoshanta. Paula wore a cool white linen dress, and Tammy wore her lime green, both girls wore hats, Paula's a floppy white one, and Tammy her one and only straw perched on top of her springing curls. The men wore check shirts and the khaki drill trousers that Tammy was beginning to recognise as almost a uniform in this part of the country.

Mixing with the crowd in the grounds, Gerry, true to his word, stuck close to Tammy. When she saw the tall figure of Rick Hatton approaching she clutched Gerry's arm. 'Now for it!' she said in a low voice.

Gerry grinned and pressed her arm against his side. 'Courage, girl,' he murmured.

Rick Hatton stood looking at them, and Tammy looked at him. He wore a fawn shirt with dark brown corded trousers—he would be different, thought Tammy. It was a second or so before he spoke. His eyes lingered deliberately on Tammy's arm tucked into Gerry's. 'So you are quite well, I see,' he drawled.

'Nice of you to find the time to attend.'

'Oh, we made a point of it, didn't we, Gerry?' Tammy replied airily, completely forgetting her docility resolution. Gerry's grin grew wider. 'Sure did,' he agreed.

Rick Hatton's lips thinned, and she knew she had put her foot in it again. For heaven's sake, she'd keep her mouth shut from now on!

He looked at Gerry. 'The boys could do with some help in getting the barrels over from the town—how about it, Gerry?' he asked softly.

Gerry was silent for a second or so, then he said slowly, 'Okay, boss.' He turned to Tammy. 'Keep me a chicken leg, will you, honey?' and he gently disengaged his arm from hers.

'Can't,' said Tammy desperately. 'I help you?'

'No, you can't,' replied Rick Hatton between clenched teeth. 'I've got something lined up for you to do,' he caught her arm none too gently and placed it through his and turned her round towards the crowd. Tammy attempted to pull away, but he only held her firmer. 'You can see lover boy later. Right now I've got just the job for you.'

They walked through the grounds to the homestead, but Tammy baulked at actually going in. Rick gave her an icy stare. 'It's work I have on my mind, so don't get any wrong ideas. When I said I didn't go for skinny types I meant it. So rest easy. You're not in my league,' he ground out.

Tammy took a deep breath. He'd said it with such

emphasis it couldn't fail to be called an insult. That did it! She was sorry for Mr Hampton, but she could get him a replacement, she wasn't staying in this high and mighty territory a day longer than she had to!

They had by now entered the house. Rick kept a hold on her arm and propelled her through to a room at the back of the house. It was an office. There was a large desk holding pride of place against one wall, and resting in the middle of it a typewriter. Rick all but threw her in the chair in front of the desk. He got a folder out and flung it down before her.

'There's some letters I want answered,' he said curtly. 'My book-keeper's still off sick. You can see the replies are pencilled in. If you can keep your mind off lover boy for an hour or so, I might have some answers to post off tomorrow. Can do?' he asked in a voice that dared her to refuse.

There must, mused Tammy, be a typists' union somewhere. It was Sunday. However, she saw no point in bringing the subject up. She glanced at him coldly.

'You will, I hope, sign the necessary form?' she asked.

His brows went up. 'What form?' he demanded.

She sighed and explained patiently, 'When we do work for any other employer—other, that is, than the one we're assigned to—we have to have special clearance. Mr Hampton is not here to agree to my doing the work, so I can't do it without your signature.'

He grinned. 'But I am your employer,' he said. 'Didn't you know? Wamanta belongs to me. Mr

50

Hampton is just managing it for me.' He enjoyed the shock he had given her. 'So get typing,' he said quietly. Before he left, he said, 'Any queries, just shout.'

Tammy took it out on the typewriter. She pounded away with such force that the carbon copies came out as bright as the original.

Rick came back just as she was finishing off the last letter. He had either timed it right, or he was working somewhere near and heard that she had finished punishing the typewriter. She placed the letters in a pile awaiting signature.

'Finished?' he asked curtly.

Tammy nodded. 'May I go now?' she inquired coldly.

He shot her a caustic look. 'He'll keep,' he said. 'You wait until I've had a look at these letters. You wouldn't want to be dragged back again if they're not right, would you?'

Tammy took a deep breath. Silently she watched him carefully read each one of the twelve letters. Then he placed them on one side. 'Good,' he said.

She walked to the door.

'Sit down,' he ordered. 'There's no hurry.'

Tammy's eyes met his defiantly and she looked at the door. 'I shouldn't,' he drawled.

She resignedly shrugged her shoulders and stood waiting. Rick sat behind the desk and pointed to the chair in front of it. Tammy slowly walked back and sat down.

'Why didn't you come to the dance?' he shot at her.

Her eyes widened. 'Didn't Paula tell you?' she asked. 'I had some letters to write.'

His eyes narrowed. 'You've been here a week, couldn't you have found time to do them before, or has Gerry been pestering you?'

Tammy sat up at that. How dared he! 'No, he has not!' she flashed out at him. 'And even if he had, it's no business of yours.'

She saw his fists clench slowly. He looked down at them. 'You've a very bad memory, haven't you?' he said. 'I thought I'd made things clear to you not so long ago. It seems I didn't get the message through.'

Tammy flushed. She knew what he was referring to.

'So,' he said softly, 'I'll tell you again. This is my territory. Gerry is more or less under my—shall we say protection? His father entrusted him to me to knock him into shape for station ownership. So you see, Miss Dainton, it is my business. By the way, if you've any hope in that direction you'd better forget them. His family's one of the oldest in Queensland and they're mighty fussy folk. I really feel they'd draw the line at an unknown typist.'

Tammy got up slowly. She had taken all she was going to take. 'Have you quite finished?' she managed to get out. 'I've got the message, thank you.' She walked to the door and kept on going until she was out of the house.

She felt the hot tears sting her lids. It just didn't make sense. It was more than pure dislike, it was persecution. Rick Hatton actually hated her. What had she done to deserve such treatment? She could well understand a clash of personalities, but this went much deeper. Suddenly she felt a touch on her arm.

'Your handbag, Miss Dainton.'

'Thank you,' said Tammy, and didn't even bother to look back at him.

Gerry found her a little later, sitting on a stump some way away from the main picnickers.

He noted her white face. 'Are you all right, Tammy?' he asked anxiously.

She managed to smile at him. She knew she had to make some excuse. 'It's the heat, Gerry, I guess I'm not used to it.'

He seemed relieved. 'You'll soon get used to it. Come and sit in the shade.'

Once he had got her settled, he found her some food. Tammy felt as if she'd choke if she attempted to eat it, but she tried anyway.

'Gerry!' rapped out that authoritative voice. 'Come and give a hand, will you?'

CHAPTER FOUR

TAMMY rang up the Agency next morning. Mr Hampton had called in and given her a few letters and various odds and ends to get on with, and left her to it while he went on his rounds.

Mr Selby, the Agency manager, listened to her request politely. 'I'm sorry to be a nuisance,' she said, 'but I've not been too well these last few days. I think it's the heat. You did warn me, didn't you? I was wondering whether it's possible to get Maisie to take over from me, and if it's still going, I'll take that fruit farm post you mentioned. I shall be sorry to leave Mr Hampton, I've no complaints in that direction.' She couldn't think of anything else to add.

Mr Selby's reception of her request relieved her instantly. 'It fits in very well, as a matter of fact,' he informed her. 'Maisie's just finished her last spell, she's been moaning about not being able to get nearer home, so this will make her day.'

Breathing a sigh of relief, Tammy asked, 'How soon, Mr Selby?'

'Er—just a minute,' he said. She heard the rustle of papers as he looked something up. 'It's Monday now—let me see, Wednesday—that suit you? You can come back on the same transport that brings Maisie out.'

'Thank you very much, Mr Selby,' replied a very grateful Tammy.

'Don't forget to get your release form signed,' he reminded her.

Putting the receiver down, she let out a pure gasp of relief, then instantly frowned. The release form. Then she remembered that Mr Hampton had signed her first week's work form, and she brightened; he could also sign the release. Then as another thought struck her, she became sombre again. She would now have to tell him.

When he appeared later that morning and asked brightly how she was getting on, it didn't make things any easier when he commented how relieved he was to have the office work off his shoulders.

She looked at him and sighed inwardly. If only things had been different!

'Mr Hampton,' she began, then finding she couldn't look directly at him, took the bull by the horns and plunged in. 'I've made arrangements to be replaced.'

He started, and stared at her. 'But I thought you were settling in nicely, girl, I had hoped to try to get you to stay on. What's wrong?'

Tammy smiled gently at him. 'As far as you are concerned, absolutely nothing,' she said quietly. 'Believe me, Mr Hampton, if things were different I'd be only too happy to stay, as it is . . .' her voice trailed off.

He looked hard at her, then walked to the window

and stood gazing out. 'It's Rick, isn't it?' he said abruptly, then turned to face her again.

Tammy nodded. So he's noticed, she thought.

He let out a loud sigh. 'I thought so. He's been riding you hard, hasn't he? The damned young fool,' he muttered.

She said nothing. Mr Hampton came and stood beside her and put a large fatherly hand on her shoulder. 'I know it's hard for you to understand, girl, but we've all noticed it, and guess we know the reason. There's not much we can do about it. He makes his own rules. Don't be too worried about it. I was hoping it would blow over, he had another go at you yesterday, didn't he?' he said quietly.

Tammy stayed silent, her lovely eyes sombre.

He nodded. 'I thought so,' then sat down beside her. 'You've heard about Mrs Hatton, I suppose?' he asked.

Once again Tammy nodded. 'She left his father, didn't she?'

Mr Hampton ran a horny hand over his knee. 'Yes,' he said abruptly, then looked at Tammy again. 'See, girl, she was English too. I worked for his dad in those days and I remember her quite well. You've got a look of her. She was small and dark too, but her eyes were brown, not the kinda lovely blue of yours.' He got up impatiently. 'Thing is, the likeness is there and Rick must have seen it.'

Tammy was silent. She looked down at her desk. It made sense at last. 'How old was Rick when it happened?' she asked.

'Fourteen,' replied Mr Hampton. 'Old enough to feel it and see what it did to his dad. He took it hard. She did try to come back, you know, but Jack Hatton's pride got in the way.'

Tammy thought about this for a while, then smiled at him. 'Thank you for telling me. I do understand now. You do see why I must go, don't you?' she said gently.

He sighed and nodded, then gave an explosive, 'Damned young fool, no call to take it out on a nice girl like you, any fool can see you're not like the other one.'

Tammy had no answer for that. 'Will you please sign my release?' she said. 'I shall be leaving on Wednesday.'

He started. 'As soon as that?' he queried.

She nodded. 'There's a relief available, you see.' She smiled at him. 'She's a Queenslander, so she's sure to be an instant success. It's suitable all round, she would have liked this post in the first place, only she'd already started another assignment.'

With a depressed air Mr Hampton had to accept the arrangement.

There was one other thing Tammy had to ask. 'Mr Hampton, would you do something else for me?' she asked. 'Don't tell Rick Hatton until after the replacement's here and I'm on my way back to Adelaide.'

He debated a moment or so about this, then looked at her sadly and made up his mind. 'It might be best at that,' he agreed.

Tammy felt like crying. She managed a smile and thanked him for agreeing to her request.

That evening on the verandah, Gerry mentioned a forthcoming event, saying Tammy must attend it. She gave Mr Hampton an anxious look as she replied, 'We'll see.' Mr Hampton held his peace.

The following day dawned bright and cloudless. It's going to be a scorcher, thought Tammy as she glanced out of her window. She listened to the familiar sounds of Esme in the kitchen and singing at the top of her voice as she prepared breakfast. The slight lowing of cattle in the distance made her eyes mist over. She had been happy there, she would miss them all, even though she had only been there for such a short period. She wondered what the next post held in store, and hoped it would be without complications. As she smoothed her cool cotton frock over her hips she realised this would be her last day. By lunch time tomorrow, with any luck she would be on her way. Packing she would leave until the evening, she decided. Not that she had much to pack. She was grateful for the advice of Mr Selby about travelling light on these assignments.

That Mr Hampton had also realised this was her last day was made plain by his gloomy expression as he sat down to join her at breakfast. Gerry had breakfasted much earlier and already left. 'I thought,' he began, 'that as it's your last day you might have some place you'd like to see. I'm prepared to take you if there is.'

Tammy laid her cup down. In his kindly way he was trying to make up for the rough treatment of Rick Hatton.

'It's very kind of you, Mr Hampton,' she said, smiling mistily at him, 'but really there's no need. It might cause a bit of speculation too, you know. I don't want anything to get in the way or go wrong at this stage.'

'Damned young fool' muttered Mr Hampton again.

The 'damned young fool' arived in person later that morning. Tammy heard the car coming up the drive, and took defensive action. She went quickly to her room and started to pack. She found she was trembling slightly, and admonished herself for her cowardly retreat.

When the knock came at her door, she almost hit the ceiling. She gazed at her case half packed, and hurriedly hid it beneath the bed. 'Yes?' she answered.

Mr Hampton's voice somewhat reassured her until she heard his request. 'Will you have a word with Mr Hatton, Tammy?'

She quailed. Had he told Rick? 'Very well,' she replied. She squared her shoulders and put her chin out. What could he do about it, anyway? Nothing.

As she passed the office door the drawling voice stopped her. 'In here, Miss Dainton.'

Going in, she found Rick Hatton alone.

'I've had a word with Mr Hampton,' he said, and Tammy tensed. Now she was for it! She flushed slightly, he gave her a hard stare and continued.

'I need your help at Wamoshanta,' he said curtly. 'As you know, my book-keeper is sick, and there's no chance of getting him back to work for at least a couple of weeks. I'm entertaining a conference party in a week's time, and it's essential I have some secretarial assistance.' He had been studying the desk top while he spoke, now he looked full at her, meeting her eyes. 'It means you'll have to stay at the homestead, of course. Danny will collect you tomorrow. Be ready and packed at eleven.' He turned to go.

Tammy's heart was pounding. Of all the bad luck!

'Could you make it the afternoon, please?' she said in a small voice.

He turned to face her, his eyes narrowed. 'Why?' he asked harshly.

Taking a deep breath, Tammy answered, 'Because my relief won't get here until twelve.'

Rick moved back into the room and stood facing her. He didn't speak for a second or so, just silently studied her. 'What relief?' he asked softly.

Tammy met his eyes squarely. 'I'm being replaced,' she said slowly. 'At my own request. The young lady is a Queenslander and a very efficient secretary. You see, she won't get here until noon, so if you could make it a little later to collect her...' her voice trailed off.

He continued to look at her. There was a smoky expression in his eyes. 'When were these arrangements made? Isn't it etiquette to first advise your employer?'

he asked smoothly.

Tammy flushed. He's just plain mad again, she thought. Now that she knew the reason for his dislike of her it helped her to hold herself in hand.

'I didn't,' she explained slowly, 'think you'd mind. In fact, I rather thought you would be relieved I was off your territory.' Her eyes sought his and held them. 'I'm booked for another assignment. Everything has been settled. I'm sure you'll find Miss Johnson a great help.' And that, thought Tammy, was that. She started to walk past him, but he caught her arm and swung her round to face him.

'Just,' he said between clenched teeth, 'like that, eh? Well, Miss Dainton, I don't like my arrangements being made for me, without, I might add, my knowledge or consent. You can just inform Miss Johnson, or whatever her name is, to stay put. I'm perfectly satisfied with my secretarial help. Do you get it?' He glared at her, then strode over to the phone and picked it up. 'On second thoughts I'll do it myself,' he grated out.

Tammy waited silently, and heard him give the operator the Agency number. He kept his eyes on her while he waited for the connection, then suddenly barked out,

'Get packed, I've decided I need that help right away. You're coming back with me.'

Tammy stared at him. He couldn't do that, could he?

He looked at her with narrowed eyes. 'What are

61

you waiting for?' he drawled.

It didn't take long for Tammy to throw the rest of her things into the case. She was hoping Mr Selby would explain about her not standing up to the heat and advise him to accept Maisie. She stood in her room hoping against hope that Rick would fling away in a vile temper back to Wamoshanta. When the imperative knock came on her door she knew she had lost the round. 'I haven't got all day, are you ready?'

As Tammy walked to the car, Mr Hampton came striding towards them. It looked as though he had been waiting to see the result of the interview. Seeing the determined expression on his face, Tammy knew he was about to tackle Rick Hatton, who was at that precise moment getting into the car. She went to meet him and put a hand on his arm, but the roar of the car starting up drowned her words.

'It's only for a week or so, Mr Hampton,' she murmured, steadily meeting his eyes, 'then I shall be back with you.'

Giving her a searching stare, he patted her arm in an almost clumsy gesture. Tammy bit her lip and got into the car.

CHAPTER FIVE

THE next few days Tammy was kept extremely busy. She had no time to ponder on the complexities of her situation. Her office was in the rear wing of the large homestead, and she had grimaced when she had first seen this arrangement. It was well away from the main section of the house, and emphasised the fact that although Rick Hatton required her services in the secretarial line, he had no wish to make any other contact with her.

The same applied to her sleeping quarters. She had been given a room next to the housekeeper's, and had her meals with the dour Scotswoman. Tammy's spirits had sunk when first introduced to Mrs Morris. She looked all that Tammy had wished she was on that first day she had arrived. Her peppery-coloured hair was drawn back in a severe-looking bun and her sombre expression was no less forbidding. However, Tammy soon found that appearances could be misleading. It was not long before Mrs Morris's dry but witty comments on life in general endeared her to Tammy.

Rick Hatton she saw only in office hours, but he made his presence felt. He was a very meticulous boss, as she already had cause to know. He would grant her so much time each morning for queries, and dictation. The feeling that he would pounce on any mistake she made made her extra sensitive, and she would sigh with relief when the morning instructions were given and he would leave. When the letters were ready for signature, or any other work needed his attention, she would have to place them on his desk in his study at the front of the house. There was a second desk in the room, and this, Tammy surmised, would belong to his book-keeper. She smiled a little; she was not going to be allowed apparently to contaminate the room, and for this she was eternally grateful, for her nerves would never stand the strain of working in close proximity with her harsh employer.

Her little office was light and airy. There was a table, two chairs, one filing cabinet and the usual office paraphernalia on the desk. She had a calendar on the wall behind her and she studiously marked off each day with a triumphant slash. Where the end of the second week appeared she had ringed it round in red. That was zero day. The book-keeper should be back at his post. On the second month she had put two red rings that signified her assignment ending. As she crossed each day off, she saw how long she had to go to the end of the whole wretched business. Another five weeks, she thought miserably one morning, studying it. The only ray she could give herself was that she would be back at Mr Hampton's for most of that period.

She was still looking at the calendar one morning

when Rick Hatton walked in. His eyes narrowed as he saw her concentration. Tammy glanced up and hastily covered the calendar with her desk folder.

He was in no hurry to leave that morning after dictation. As usual he was not kindly disposed towards her, if anything he seemed more edgy. Tammy knew he had entertained a young lady to dinner the previous evening, Mrs Morris had informed her of the occasion. She had even described the luscious redhead. Shaking her head, she murmured, 'It's time he settled down, if you ask me.' Tammy had raised her brows at this. 'Who'd take him on?' she queried sarcastically. Mrs Morris's own brows raised at this. 'Who wouldn't, more like,' she said. 'He's wealthy, good-looking,' she gave Tammy a wicked grin, 'and has what I believe is termed by the youngsters of today as sex appeal,'

Tammy was amazed. 'Mrs Morris!' she exclaimed.

Breaking out into her deep chuckle that seemed to come up from her feet, Mrs Morris replied, 'Tammy Dainton, I believe you're more old-fashioned than I am!' Tammy burst out laughing herself at this bald statement.

Tammy now sat in her small office patiently waiting for Rick to go. He knew it, and it made him more inclined to linger if only to annoy her.

'Tell me,' he drawled, 'why did you come out here? For experience? Or to find a rich husband? Wasn't there anyone at home? Or did you leave some poor devil back there'

He was being deliberately provocative, and Tammy

65

knew it. She thought of Jonathan. Anyone less like a poor devil than Jonathan was hard to imagine. She gave him a glance of pure dislike. Well, he hated her anyway so she might as well give him something to chew on.

'Actually,' she began confidentially, noting with pleasure the small start he gave at her tone, 'there were two. You know how it is when a girl can't choose between riches and love in a garret.' His eyes narrowed, and Tammy carried on recklessly, warming to her theme. 'Now that you've put the damper on my scheme with Gerry, I'll have to rethink. A pity really, I did take a real shine to him,' she sighed elaborately. 'Oh well, there's plenty more fish in the sea—or rather,' she gave what she hoped was a roguish look, 'rich ranchers,' she frowned in concentration. 'I did hear about an old man in the North-West, absolutely loaded, needs a housekeeper. I rather thought . . .'

Rick jumped up. 'That's enough!' he shouted. 'By heaven, I was right about you all along. If you think I'm standing by and see some poor devil caught as my father was, you can think again. I'll make damned certain you never get another job this side of Australia!' and he turned to go.

Tammy grinned; she hadn't enjoyed herself so much for what seemed like years. She spoke to his departing back. 'There's something about a masterful man I go for. It's a pity you're not dark, I never cared for blond men.' Her voice gave a good imitation of his soft drawl.

66

He turned and looked back at her, his eyes blazing. He took one step towards her. Tammy didn't move, her cheeks were flushed but her eyes sparkled. Then Rick pulled himself up short. She saw a muscle move at the side of his mouth, and guessed the inward struggle he was having to get himself under control. Then he turned and flung out of the office.

Tammy almost laughed out loud. Just for once she had got the upper hand, and it was a lovely feeling. She had no regrets. It had been worth every moment. She supposed they would have agencies in New Zealand.

At supper that evening she thought she had better warn Mrs Morris that in all probability she would be leaving in the morning. Mrs Morris gave her a searching look. 'Was it you that upset him this morning?' she queried. 'He's been fit to chew nails most of the day.' Tammy chuckled, and nodded. Mrs Morris looked worried. 'Be careful, Tammy,' she said. 'That's one man that likes his own way. Just you remember that.'

Tammy was so certain she would receive her marching orders that she was packed and ready by the time she reached her office the following morning. She had even gone so far as to carry her case down with her and place it with her coat in the small annexe leading into the room.

When Rick sauntered in at nine-thirty, he gave her case a cursory glance and looked back at her. 'Going somewhere?' he said softly. 'I'm afraid you're going to be disappointed, Miss Dainton. You can take that case back again after our little talk.' He settled himself opposite her and reached in his pocket for a cigarette, then lighting up, watched the smoke spiral upwards with narrowed eyes. Tammy eyed him warily, noting the strong line of his jaw and the well moulded lips now firmly set.

'You aired your ambitions to the wrong person, you know,' he drawled. 'In other words, Miss Dainton, your treasure hunt is over—on this continent anyway. I'm keeping you.' He looked straight at her and there was an unpleasant glint in his eyes. 'I've made the necessary arrangements with the Agency. You're here for your whole stay in Australia. Two years, isn't it?' His smile could not be called pleasant either.

Tammy stared at him. Her eyes opened wide. Then the enormity of what he had done hit her.

'I'll break my agreement, then!' she stormed at him.

He looked at her. 'I'll sue the Agency for all they've got if you do,' he said calmly.

Looking at his grim face, Tammy knew he would do just that. She thought back. She had signed on with the Agency for two years, that was correct, but she had some rights, didn't she? It was no use asking him to wait until she found out what they were. No use pleading with him either. He'd rather like that, she thought with clenched teeth. She looked down at her hands now closed into small fists.

'I've read the agreement pretty thoroughly,' he went on softly. 'There's no way you can back out, except by putting the Agency in the red. Oh, there is one way it can be broken.' His eyes met Tammy's as she glanced up quickly at him. 'By marriage,' he said slowly, 'but that, Miss Dainton, is just not on the cards, I'll see to that.'

For some time after he had left, Tammy sat shell-shocked. She shook her head. He just couldn't do that. He was bluffing. The phone rang; she picked it up, and the mocking tones of Rick Hatton came over the wire. 'Mr Selby wants to have a word with you, Miss Dainton. I'm putting him through now.'

Feeling she had been saved by the bell, Tammy spoke tremulously. 'Mr Selby?'

'Good morning, Miss Dainton. Well, well, I'm mighty proud of you,' he said.

'You are?' Tammy said faintly.

'Sure am,' he replied jovially. 'You've broken the existing record for long service with your first assignment. I must say Mr Hatton's sure impressed with you, he's signed you up for your whole period, and I've a feeling he's got something in line for you after that.'

Tammy felt unwell. She was sure he had. 'Er . . . Mr Selby, is everything signed and sealed?' she asked hopefully.

'It most certainly is,' he said happily. 'I'm looking at his cheque right now and I must say he's been pretty generous. You'll find your rates, young lady,

69

are a lot higher than we agreed. You can thank Mr Hatton for that. He's taken on the payment of your cheque, by the way. Well, congratulations again. Don't hesitate to call on me, if you want me any time. The Agency is mighty grateful to you,' and he rang off.

She was still sitting holding the receiver in a dazed condition when the smooth voice said, 'Satisfied, Miss Dainton?'

Tammy tore up the calendar. She wanted no reminders of the long months ahead. She still couldn't really take it in. Surely he must have known she had not meant a word of that ridiculous tarradiddle she had come out with? Her lips tightened. He had believed it because he had wanted to believe it. As mad as it sounded, she was being made to pay for something that had happened a long time ago.

She spoke little at supper time. Mrs Morris glanced at her once or twice, but decided not to probe, and Tammy was grateful for her thoughtfulness. After supper, she wandered out into the grounds. It was cool in the evening light. Soon she knew it would be quite dark. It would happen suddenly, she would never get used to this sudden fall of night. She sighed; she had time enough now to get used to it.

She walked on. The scent of the oleanders gently wafted on the breeze as she passed their blossom-laden bushes. She gazed upwards; the stars, much larger than the ones seen at home, twinkled away in a world of their own. There was peace all around her as she stood facing the paddock, leaning on the white post of the fence. Peace was far from her thoughts. She had escaped Jonathan's net only to fall into another. A horse whinnied not far away. Had she startled it? Or was there someone else close by? The thought that it might be Rick Hatton made her abruptly turn and begin the return journey. She had no wish to meet him.

On the Monday morning she was coldly informed that he was entertaining a few business acquaintances from the conference that evening, and she was to act as hostess. Tammy's eyes opened wide. He gave her a caustic look.

'Serve drinks and refreshments and generally make yourself useful. You may also be called upon in the office capacity—all purely business, I can assure you, Miss Dainton. There's just one thing I'd like you to remember, you are not out to impress anyone, which I must admit will be rather frustrating for you, as there will be at least three rich ranchers present.'

Tammy felt there was no point in answering. Rick smiled at her silence and walked away.

'Not out to impress anyone!' fumed Tammy later, as she began to get ready for her enforced evening's stint. He had no conscience about making her work in what should be her time off. She stared at her reflection in the mirror and saw a slim, almost wraith-like girl staring back at her. Rick had called her 'skinny'. She held her head on one side. Was she? Then she sighed. Jonathan had called her his 'pocket Venus'. Well, she thought wryly, you couldn't please everyone. Then she frowned : what on earth should she wear? A phrase went through her mind : 'The hostess with the mostest'. She grimaced, she could hardly be called that! She went through her scanty wardrobe, and her fingers touched the gossamer folds of her 'You never know' dress, an evening dress bought on the advice of Maisie when asked what she would need for the assignment. 'I always take a "you never know" dress,' Maisie solemnly told Tammy. 'I was asked out once to a fabulous do and hadn't a thing to wear, I'm never going to get caught like that again.'

Tammy went back to the dress. She took it out and stared at it, and the frown was slowly replaced by an unholy grin. She could almost picture Rick Hatton's embarrassment when she floated in wearing it. If nothing else was meant to impress, this dress was. Its colouring was sea green, specked with tiny gold threads that caught the light. The gossamer folds floated out below her waist. The thin shoulder straps served no other purpose than for decoration, as the dress fitted sheathlike above her waist. With a determined expression she laid it out on the bed. Next she attended to her hair. This she piled up on the top of her head, Grecian style, and secured it with a gold band. Finally she slipped the dress on. When she surveyed the finished result, she shuddered. Rick would hit the roof! But, she told herself, it was going to be worth it. She knew he was going to entertain every night that week. Just stick this one evening out, she told herself, he's not likely to ask for a repeat performance.

Her knees were decidedly weak by the time she put in an appearance. One glance at Rick Hatton as she entered the large room told her all she needed to know about his reaction. His jaw squared and his eyes were like chipped ice. His gaze travelled slowly over her from top to bottom. Not a detail was missed. Tammy flushed but stood her ground. There were about fifteen men present, wearing, Tammy noted in some relief, white shirts and dark trousers, what could almost be called evening wear. The talk stopped abruptly on her entry, and she felt every eye upon her. Devoutly wishing the floor would open up and swallow her, she waited awkwardly by the door.

Rick Hatton crossed the room and stood beside her, introducing her to his colleagues. 'My secretary, Miss Dainton,' he murmured. 'If anyone's short of a drink she'll supply it.' He turned to Tammy. 'Well, get weaving, the drinks are over there.'

Tammy knew as much about keeping a bar as she did about jet flying, but she had no choice in the matter. A rotund gentleman who introduced himself as Ned Castle advised her to circle the guests and inquire their poison. She thanked him and started to do just that. At least that was the idea when she started out, but she found she was constantly being held up by interested if not downright curious acquaintances of Rick Hatton. The fact that she was English was an added attraction. Tammy found herself giving the same answers as she had given Mr Hampton, well aware of Rick Hatton's watchful eyes on her.

A tall bronzed man around the forty mark took more than a casual interest in her. Tammy could feel his eyes following her every move, and she didn't like the look she saw in them. He had a very pronounced southern drawl, and she was certain he was one of the rich ranchers Rick Hatton had referred to earlier. Without being obvious about it, she kept her distance. Snatches of conversation about grazing rights, mineral rights and water bores were all above her head and she by-passed these earnest gentlemen. If they wanted a drink they knew where to come, she thought, as she stationed herself beside the drinks table. The first to seek her out was the bronzed man. She had half expected it. He had curiously light brown eyes.

'Name's Dan Everly,' he said abruptly. 'Yours?'

'Miss Dainton,' murmured Tammy.

His eyebrows rose a fraction. 'Don't stand on ceremony, honey, we're friendly people, you know,' he drawled. 'Could get friendlier if given a bit of encouragement.' The light brown eyes rested on her bare shoulders. 'Friend of Rick's?' he queried.

Tammy blushed. She had a pretty good idea what he was getting at. 'Secretary, full stop,' she said coldly.

He grinned, and Tammy decided she didn't like his smile either. 'Rick's slipping, then,' he drawled. 'How much is he paying you?'

He had, thought Tammy, gone far enough. 'What

74

would you like to drink, Mr Everly?' she asked quietly.

His eyes narrowed and he moved closer to her. 'What I'd like is definitely not in the drinks line.'

She stiffened as his arm crept around her waist.

'Being well looked after, Dan?' asked Rick Hatton.

Dan Everly did not remove his arm from Tammy as he answered. 'I've decided I need a secretary, Rick,' then looked back at Tammy. 'Whatever he's paying you I'll double it.'

'Nothing doing,' drawled Rick Hatton. 'This one is special, if you know what I mean. You ought to know by now that I never share my women.'

Tammy stiffened. Of all the insults he had given, veiled or not, this was the worst! Her blazing eyes met his bland ones. Her cheeks felt red hot.

The arm dropped reluctantly from her waist. 'Remember the name, honey, if you want a change,' Dan Everly murmured.

Feeling sick, Tammy brushed past the two men. She heard Rick Hatton's imperative 'Miss Dainton', but she kept on going. Enough was enough, and she had just about had it. She didn't even feel sorry for the Agency, they should have checked with her first. As long as they had the money they didn't care if she had been sold into white slavery, and that, she told herself, fuming, as she reached her bedroom and got her case out and started flinging her things into it, was just what this assignment was turning into.

The hard rap on her door did not deter her. 'Who

is it?' she asked coldly, knowing full well who it would be. She glanced at the door—was there a key? she might need it. There was no key.

'Are you coming out, or do I come in?' was the curt request.

'I've gone to bed,' shouted Tammy. 'And don't you dare come in, I'm not decent.'

Not that that, thought Tammy, would stop Rick Hatton. Surprisingly it did.

'Well, get decent, and come to the study. At once, do you hear?' he shouted. 'I'll give you five minutes.'

Tammy's heart thudded. She could go into Mrs Morris's room for protection, but Mrs Morris took sleeping tablets, so she would first have to rouse her to gain that protection; then she straightened and stuck her chin out. She wasn't afraid of that great bully, was she? No, she told herself, just plain terrified! She closed her eyes. She had better go and get it over with. He was not going to get away with insulting her like that.

She took her time, but eventually she had to go in. He was standing by the desk and looked like thunder.

'Shut the door,' he commanded. 'We don't want to be overheard, do we?'

'Why not?' said Tammy loudly. 'They'll know sooner or later. It may be the first time in history, but one of your women is leaving you high and dry, Rick Hatton. I'll take so much, but I draw the line at being classed in that society. Sue the Agency, I don't care. I'm leaving in the morning, I'll get back to town if I have to walk it!'

'Finished?' he drawled.

'Yes, thank you,' she said politely, and turned to go.

'Well, I haven't,' he said grimly, and barred her from the door. 'Now you listen to me, spitfire. You asked for what happened out there.' His eyes rested on her shoulders. 'What did you expect? They're men, you know, not boys. You can come in every night looking like Venus rising out of the waves, but no prince is going to carry you off on a white charger, I can personally guarantee that. After what I said tonight no man will molest you again. You are now known as my property, and that counts for something around here. There will be no further offers. Understand?'

Tammy did understand. Her blazing eyes met the cold grey ones, she slipped past him, but he hadn't finished with her. He caught her arm.

'In case you still haven't got the message, I want you to take a few cold facts into consideration before you fly back to town. Suing the Agency will only be the start of things. I'll see your name splashed across every paper in Southern Australia and I've the influence to do it. I could also give a very revealing interview about our relationship, after tonight,' his glance flicked once again over her bare shoulders, 'who wouldn't believe it? It would be my word against yours, and my word, Miss Dainton, would hold good.'

Tammy's eyes closed. It didn't bear thinking about.

'Having second thoughts?' he murmured.

Her eyes were huge as they met his. 'Do you know what you're doing?' she whispered. 'You're punishing me for what happened years ago, aren't you?'

He shrugged. 'Perhaps,' he said. 'But you've shown me what you are. I've no regrets. I must say I was surprised at your show of squeamishness tonight,' he said harshly. 'Or was it that you didn't like others knowing what you were?' He leaned closer to her as he said this. Tammy shrank back from him. She hated him—it was in her eyes. Rick laughed and pulled her towards him.

'There's something about you when you look like that that I can't resist,' he said, and held her chin in an iron grip, forcing her head against the door. She twisted wildly, realising what was coming, but it was useless. For the second time she felt the bruising hurt of his lips. When she was weak and breathless, his lips traced the curve of her neck and moved slowly along her shoulder. 'You know,' he murmured, 'I could get to like this.' He laughed as he felt her shudder, then released her abruptly. 'But like I said, you're not in my class. Go to bed, gold-digger.'

CHAPTER SIX

TAMMY reached her room still in a daze. She leaned weakly back against the door, then shook her head. It just couldn't be happening! She walked slowly over to the bed and sat down. Her lips still hurt and she could still feel the touch of his lips on her shoulder. She shuddered. What a blind fool she had been! Rick had been right when he had said she had asked for it. Her lips thinned; all she had wanted to do was defy him, and where had it got her? Deeper into the morass.

Angrily she shrugged herself out of the dress. She would not be wearing that again. That Rick still expected her to attend further sessions was obvious. She would wear her grey dress. It was quite plain, long-sleeved and with its little white peter pan collar looked almost quakerish. It would at least discourage a repetition of what she had just been through. She thought of Rick's threats. They were ridiculous, but even as she tried to convince herself of this fact, she felt a touch of fear; in everyone else's sight, he was a sober, well respected, not to mention wealthy member of society. And he had said, it would be his word against hers. The thought of his 'revealing interview' made her blood run cold. That he would go through with it she had no doubt. Rick Hatton was not a person to make empty threats. She would not stand a chance. Not here, not even with Mr Hampton's help, who she felt sure would stand by her. She passed a hand over her forehead. What a mess: From now on she would have to watch her every step, make Rick think he had succeeded in browbeating her. There would be a chance to get out some time in the future, and Tammy wanted out, fast. She had no intention of spending two years in this environment.

Apart from coffee, Tammy abstained at breakfast the following morning. Mrs Morris was too busy preparing delicacies for the evening's guests to notice her dejection. At nine sharp Tammy wandered down to her office and gave everything a cursory dust over to relieve Mrs Morris of that one duty, then had another try at opening her window; it had stuck two days before, and Tammy had forgotten to mention it to Mrs Morris to have it fixed. She gave it one last exasperated pull without success and was about to turn away when an arm brushed hers and gave the frame a heavy thump. It loosened immediately and was pushed up.

Tammy turned and looked at Rick Hatton. He wore what Tammy would, had she been back home, have called town wear. His suit of dark grey was immaculate and the pink shirt and dark grey tie, a match for the suit, highlighted his blond colouring. He acknowledged her stare with slightly narrowed eyes. When he spoke, his voice held its customary coldness.

'I shall be out until three,' he nodded to the filing cabinet. 'You'll find some old files at the back, get out new ones for them and label them. That should keep you busy. If you're at a loose end, you can always help Mrs Morris. I shall in all probability have some work for you when I return.' He nodded curtly and left.

Tammy stared after him. In other words, be around when I get back, or else, she thought.

Danny came in at eleven to fix the window. He gave it a brief examination and muttered something about slicing a little off, then grinned at Tammy. 'Sure do get around, don't you? Looks,' he said slyly, 'as if you got the job after all.'

Tammy was not amused, and her expression said so.

'Come on,' teased Danny, 'don't tell me you're the only female who hasn't fallen for the boss.'

Tammy's eyes smouldered. 'You wouldn't believe me if I did,' she said, crashing the filing cabinet open, thinking bitterly why she couldn't have one day of peace without the subject of Rick Hatton being forced on her.

Danny squatted on his heels and searched in his tool bag for what he wanted. 'Okay,' he muttered, 'so he gave you the brush-off. You sure don't look the type to hold a grudge,' he said.

Tammy was speechless. Danny started chipping at the frame. 'Tell you what,' he said in between chips, 'have a bet with you, you'll be eating out of his hand inside three months.'

'If,' said Tammy in a low voice, 'he held out his hand to me I'd bite it!' It was said with such force that Danny stood almost open-mouthed staring at her.

'Say, he did get your goat, didn't he?'

Tammy was suddenly sick of the whole conversation. Danny was only passing the time. He didn't understand, there was no reason to take it out on him. She felt her eyes stinging, and turned back hastily to the cabinet. Danny still stood there. He had not missed the tears.

'So that's what's wrong with Joe Hampton,' he muttered. 'He's been asking every day how you were. I kinda thought he was taking a bit more interest in you than was called for.' He pushed his old hat off his forehead. 'Well, I'll be durned,' he said. 'I've been kinda slow, haven't I?'

Tammy said nothing. She still wasn't sure what Danny meant, if he really knew. His next words gave the answer.

His pale blue eyes burned with an intensity that slightly alarmed Tammy. 'What's he think Rick's going to do with you?' he demanded. 'As if he don't know that boy as well as I do. Wouldn't harm a hair on anyone's head. Getting soft, I reckon,' he said scathingly.

Tammy bristled, quick in defence of her one and only friend. 'Perhaps he's a bit more observant than most people,' she suggested.

Danny flung down the tool and Tammy had a feeling he would like to stamp on it. Instead he threw off his hat as well. His wiry hair seemed to stand on end. 'Okay,' he grated out. ''Cos he don't give no fancy talk and acts a bit sharp like, that don't mean he means you any harm.'

Tammy had the answer to that, but remained silent.

'I've heard the talk all right,' went on Danny. 'I don't pay no mind to it. Got nothing else to do, some folk. They say he's got a down on you 'cos you're English.'

Tammy met his eyes squarely. 'It happens to be true,' she shrugged. 'I don't know what actually happened all those years ago, but it does appear to have gone to his head,' she finished bitterly.

'Now you ain't giving Rick no fair hearing,' he burst out.

Tammy's eyes opened wide. 'Ain't—' she corrected herself hastily. 'Not giving him a fair hearing indeed! I suppose he's giving me one!'

Danny shook his head. 'Seems to me you two get on like a couple of fighting Abos. As for going to his head, I'd like to meet the nipper whose head it wouldn't have gone to. He fair idolised his dad. As for his ma—well, she weren't his real ma. She passed over when he were a real nipper. Jack Hatton took this second one when Rick were eight. As for her, she had no time for Rick, no time for anyone 'cept

83

herself. The station weren't what it is today. They were struggling in those days. She were English, as I said. I don't know how Jack Hatton met her, but he'd upped and married her in a month, and she not knowing much about life out here, thought she were on to a good thing, thought because he owned a station she were in clover. Got quite a shock, she did, when she moved from Adelaide up here, let everybody know it too. There was no doubt about it, she were just a good-timer, out for what she could get. Pretty as a picture too, and all fresh-looking.'

He looked sadly at Tammy and nodded. 'Guess she looked a bit like you at that,' he sighed, and continued. 'Well, his dad never took her to heel. He was crazy about her, she could do no wrong. I guess in time he'd have tamed her, if that blamed jackaroo hadn't turned up. The minute she learned his folk had cash she made a dead set at him, then they lit.' He shook his head. 'Jack Hatton never got over it. Rick tried to help,' his pale blue eyes moistened. 'How he tried, he were only a lad, but he tried. Fair broke my heart to watch. His dad took to the bottle. Rick had to grow up fast and he did.' He stared moodily at Tammy. 'You said it went to his head, guess it went to his heart too.'

Tammy sat down and gazed blindly at the wall. She vaguely wondered whether the deep scar inside Rick Hatton would ever heal. Not while she was around. She thought of the day she had deliberately baited him, of what she had said about Gerry. Gerry

84

was a jackaroo. But how could she possibly have known? Recalling his look and the effort he had had to make to keep his hands off her, she marvelled at his self-control, he must have dearly wanted to throttle her.

She looked at Danny bending to pick up his tool. 'Thank you, Danny,' she said quietly. 'I can understand a lot better now.'

Danny grunted and got on with fixing the window.

A sedately dressed and much subdued Tammy circulated the guests that evening. Speaking only when spoken to, she drifted amongst them, seeing to their wants. If she stayed overlong talking to a particular man, it would not be long before Rick Hatton joined them. He was making certain she realised her position.

In spite of her reticence one young man constantly hovered. She was just handing a drink to a waiting guest when she glanced up to catch his eye on her. Then he smiled, showing even white teeth. It was such a pleasant smile that Tammy found herself smiling back at him. The next thing she knew Rick Hatton was beside her and had placed a casual arm round her waist as she bent to pick up a bottle. Tammy nearly dropped the bottle. 'Let me go' she grated in a low voice.

'When I'm ready,' was the soft answer. Then, 'Can you manage, honey?' he drawled loudly.

Tammy knew she was being punished for smiling at the young man. Even though she knew the cause behind her persecution it was hard to be sympathetic when on the receiving end.

Tammy thought things were bad enough and never dreamed they could get worse, but they did. The following evening something happened that she would not have thought possible. By now she had mastered the art of hostessing and could accept up to four orders without mixing them up, and the evening was well advanced when a late arrival turned up. Tammy felt him stare at her and it did not particularly bother her, she was getting used to such interest. When he thanked her for the drink she had handed him, she noted with some surprise that he was English. Suddenly he snapped his fingers. 'Got you!' he exclaimed.

Tammy started. He looked at her and smiled. 'It's been worrying me ever since I walked in,' he said. Tammy's eyebrows lifted. She had no idea who the man was.

'Jonathan Drew,' he announced triumphantly.

Tammy thought she was going to faint. Quickly she spoke to him before Rick Hatton came into ear-shot.

'How is he?' she asked.

'Don't you know?' he laughed. 'The name's Bolton, by the way—Nick. You wouldn't remember me. I do business now and again with Drew. You were at a wine and cheese party at the Savoy last year.'

Tammy could feel Rick Hatton's eyes on her. 'I haven't heard from him lately,' she said hastily. 'Is there anything else I can get you, Mr Bolton?' She did not linger long after that. Just how friendly was he with Jonathan? If he ever got to hear about this, she thought, he would drag her to the altar on the grounds that she wasn't fit to look after herself. He'd hinted as much before she had left. Tammy bit her lip. It was one chance in a thousand that someone who knew Jonathan would turn up there, but it had happened.

At the close of the evening Mr Bolton sought her out again. He said he hoped to see her again before he left Australia, he was due to fly back to England on the Sunday. Tammy was on tenterhooks lest he ask if she had any message for Jonathan. Out of the corner of her eye she had noticed Rick Hatton nearby. He must have heard Mr Bolton's request to see her again. Tammy played safe, and answered that she hoped it would be possible too.

Rick Hatton escorted him to the door and went outside with him. Her hands clenched. He was after information. He had not missed a thing.

Halfway to her room a short while later, his voice stopped her. 'I want a word with you,' he said curtly.

Tammy turned and looked at him. 'I'm tired,' she said. 'Can't it wait until tomorrow?'

He pointed to the study door. Tammy sighed and retraced her steps.

Rick closed the door and stood looking at her.

'Who is Jonathan Drew?' he asked harshly.

Tammy gave a start. Her nails dug into her palms.

'Well?' he repeated.

'Someone I once knew,' said Tammy lamely.

'I gathered that much,' he grated. 'How well?'

'That is purely personal,' said Tammy, making an effort tired as she was to stand her ground.

He walked slowly towards her. 'Do I have to shake it out of you?' he said softly. 'Because I intend to know. Do you want more of the other evening's treatment?' He pulled her to him with a force that knocked the breath out of her.

Tammy was quite decided on this point. 'I'll tell you,' she said breathlessly.

He laughed at her reaction and released her. She walked away from him, trying to marshal her thoughts. How to begin? Not that he'd understand any of it.

'He—he wanted to marry me,' she said slowly; her eyes met his, the sardonic look in his was not lost on her.

'One man's meat,' he drawled.

Tammy flushed. There wasn't much point in going on.

'That's all there is to it,' she said firmly.

'Oh no, you don't,' he said quickly. 'There's a darn sight more than that, I know. You got engaged, then cleared off and left him, didn't you? Which was the poor devil? The rich man or the poor one?'

'Mind your own business!' flashed out Tammy, stung to unwise repartee.

He took a quick step towards her. 'You never learn, do you?'

Tammy flinched back against a low chair and found

herself sinking into it. She held up her hand quickly.

'All right,' she said wearily. 'Rich man, if you want it put that way.'

'What happened? Was he old? Did you suddenly realise what marriage meant? He must have been repulsive to put you off the money stakes,' he jeered.

Tammy felt she had only disliked Rick Hatton before because she really hated him now. What right had he to take the past out of her? Jonathan loved her. He was worth six of this bullying, sarcastic type.

She stood up, fire flashed from her eyes and her cheeks were flushed. 'For your information,' she said, finding it hard to control her voice she was so angry. 'Jonathan is in his early thirties. He is extremely good-looking, dark, with blue eyes,' she noted with pleasure the small start he had given. 'You said I was not in your league,' she added bitterly. 'You don't know how right you were. Jonathan could teach you how to treat a woman. I ought to have married him. I miss him.' The last words came out slowly. Tammy was all played out. Quite suddenly it just wasn't worth it. Remembering Jonathan had made her homesick, she wanted her room and solitude. Tonight she would do what this man had advised her to do on that first punishing occasion—cry into her pillow. She did not even look at Rick Hatton. Her head was low. 'May I go now?' she asked wearily.

She was entirely unprepared for his next move. He walked towards her and lifted her head and looked into her eyes. 'So I don't know how to treat a woman,

Miss Dainton? Well now, that all depends on the woman. If I felt attracted to her,' his eyes fell on her lips. Tammy made a convulsive movement away from him. He brought his arm round her waist so that she could not move further back. This time his movements were not forceful but gentle, nevertheless firm. 'I said if,' he said softly. 'My kisses would not punish, they would speak.' He bent his head towards her, and Tammy struggled to free herself. 'Please don't,' she begged desperately. 'You can't prove anything to me, I don't want to know.'

Before his lips met hers, he murmured, 'But you are going to know. You've issued a challenge, and I never ignore a challenge.'

Tammy winced, waiting for the bruising hurt of his lips, but they were as soft as thistledown at first, then slowly but exorably more firm and insistent. He was perfectly right, thought Tammy, going under in a maze of moons and stars, they did speak, and the message they gave was as old as the hills.

She was trembling from head to foot when at last he released her. Her wide eyes met his mocking ones. 'Satisfied?' he drawled softly. Tammy ran for cover.

Reaching her room, she threw herself on the bed and the tears she had held back for so long cascaded down her face. Homesickness was only part of her sorrow. Some time during that kiss she had had to acknowledge the bitter-sweet realisation that she was in love with a man who hated her. It had reached through to her as he had held her in that all-enveloping warmth of his arms.

Her tears spent, she lay back and gazed out at the velvety darkness beyond the bedroom window. The brilliant stars were still twinkling their message of peace. She thought how desperately she had wanted to throw her arms round his neck and cling to him, to tell him it didn't matter whether he hated her or not as long as he held her like that, she would never leave him. She shook her head. That was pure madness. Had she lost her pride? Could she take two years of coldness and hurt? The tears rolled down her cheek and she shook them away. More hurt should he ever realise she loved him. He would play on it. For him it would be a kind of justification for what he had been through all those years ago. She got up wearily and pushed back her hair off her forehead with a tired gesture. Heaven forbid he should ever know it.

CHAPTER SEVEN

AT breakfast next morning, Mrs Morris gave her a sharp look. 'You look as if you've not been sleeping too well,' she commented in her forthright way.

'I think I'm homesick, Mrs Morris,' Tammy replied with a wry grimace. 'Funny, really, I've no people left at home. Dad was all I had, and he died a year ago.'

'It's still home,' said Mrs Morris, filling up her cup. 'I've been here so long, this is home.' She sat down and picked up her cup. 'Mind you, when I come to think of it, I got homesick often. No cure really, you have to wait till it wears off.'

Tammy looked at her. She had never said much about her personal life. 'Did you immigrate with your family?' she asked.

Mrs Morris shook her head and smoothed down her spotless apron. 'Just me and Mr Morris,' she said, then added abruptly, 'Had a son. Lost him in the bombing.' Tammy wished she hadn't asked. Mrs Morris finished her tea and started to clear the table, as if she suddenly needed something to do, then spoke again. 'Reason we came, really. I couldn't seem to pull myself together. Tom thought a new life away from familiar surroundings might help.' She looked with unseeing eyes at the gleaming kitchen range. 'It didn't. Not for a long time anyway.' She looked back at Tammy. 'It wants thinking about, you know. You're young enough to go back when you've had enough. Time you settled down, too. Got a fellow back there?'

Tammy shook her head. There was of course Jonathan, but she didn't want to marry him, so it was the truth.

Mrs Morris's words echoed in her mind as she sat in her small office later that morning, 'Go home.' Her fingers stilled on the keys of the typewriter. Why shouldn't she? Rick Hatton was only concerned about his own countrymen. Her thoughts raced on. It was her only hope. She must leave as soon as possible.

As she sat taking dictation, she studied his cold profile—he rarely looked directly at her while dictating. He would stare out at the paddocks, and she noted how his eyes would narrow slightly as he concentrated in thought. For all the notice he took of her, she might have been an answering machine, she thought bitterly. When he was through, he got up to go.

'Mr Hatton,' Tammy spoke quickly before her courage deserted her, 'could I have a word with you?'

'Well?' he said coldly.

Tammy swallowed. 'I want to go home to England,' she said quickly. 'I promise to take the first boat out if you'll release me.'

The silence that followed tautened Tammy's nerves. He continued to stare at her.

'Back to Jonathan?' he said sardonically.

Tammy couldn't look at him. 'Yes,' she said in a low voice.

When she next glanced at him, his eyes were narrowed and there was a white line about his mouth. She felt her pulse rate rise. She was beginning to know the signs.

'You didn't think I believed your fairy story last night, did you?' he said harshly. 'If he's the paragon of virtue that you claim, apart from being wealthy, that is, I really can't see him waiting around for you. Some other designing female would have snapped him up. I should forget it if I were you.' He walked to the door, then turned back to her. 'I paid well for your services, Miss Dainton. What recompense could you offer if, and I mean if, I agree?'

Tammy looked at him. 'You would be paid back every penny,' she said quietly.

He smiled unpleasantly. 'Jonathan again, I presume?'

Tammy made one last try. 'Please,' she said pleadingly.

His lips thinned. 'You are going nowhere, Miss Dainton. Get that into your head once and for all, and cut out the violin stuff, it just won't work.'

Before he closed the door he barked out, 'I want those letters before lunch,' and slammed it shut.

Tammy was left wondering how it was possible to love and hate a person at the same time. It did occur to her several times that week that she had only to let

Jonathan know where she was and he would be there, but her heart baulked at the thought. It would be admitting defeat and into another situation it would be difficult to extricate herself from. She did not see Mr Bolton again. She had no means of knowing whether he had tried to get into contact with her. She was grateful to him for not supplying Rick Hatton with the information he had obviously sought. He would not have had to pump her if he had been successful.

The conference had ended and Tammy's evenings were now her own. Paula had rung her up on the Saturday morning. Tammy had guessed what she was going to ask her, and had to refuse. She could not risk another confrontation over Gerry. If she went to the dance she could not very well ignore him, and she was going to be very careful not to do anything that might invite another of Rick Hatton's devastating retaliatory acts. She promised Paula she would try and make it the following week. Things, she felt, were getting impossible.

It was Mrs Morris's weekend off and she had already left to visit friends in Adelaide. There was plenty of food in the Frigidaire, she had informed Tammy the previous evening. Rick Hatton, Tammy learnt, spent the weekends visiting the outstations, and was rarely around. This news had been greeted with relief by Tammy. She did not mind spending the two days alone. She planned several walks. The station ran for miles, and as yet she hadn't seen much of it apart from the homestead grounds.

After a solitary breakfast she sorted out a lunch pack and was just going to collect her hat when she met Rick Hatton coming out of his study. She was somewhat surprised, sure that he would have left by then. He stood and gave her a caustic inspection. Tammy suffered it in silence. Dressed in jeans and T-shirt, she knew she looked vastly different from the cool secretarial image she had been careful to impose. Her diminutive five foot two was more pronounced in sneakers. In her day shoes the heels helped supplement her lack of height. She hadn't even bothered to pin her hair back and it hung loose about her shoulders. Her wide violet eyes took in his appearance at the same time. The cream shirt and khaki slacks had been replaced by a navy blue short-sleeved shirt and tan slacks. She noticed the fair hairs on his chest showing in the open neck, and hastily averted her eyes.

'You did say twenty-two, didn't you?' he demanded, 'You look sixteen.' His eye then caught the lunch pack. 'Where are you going?'

Tammy was still smarting from his previous remark. It was a touchy subject with her, for she had always gone to great pains to look her age. She thought of his question. How on earth did she know where she was going? 'Round and about,' she answered airily.

He did not like that reply. He took a step towards her, and Tammy backed hastily. 'I don't know where,' she explained quickly. 'I just thought I'd go walking.'

He had not missed the hasty step back. 'That's better,' he drawled softly. 'I did wonder how long you'd keep up the docility act. At least we now know where we stand, don't we, Miss Dainton?'

Tammy said nothing, and wished he would go.

'What,' he suddenly demanded, 'happens when you go through a gate?'

Tammy stared at him. 'What gate?' she queried.

He gave a snort, 'I thought so!' then glared at her. 'For your information I'm talking about cattle gates. You can't miss them. Well, you close them after you. Get it?'

She nodded.

He gave a heavy sigh. 'No, I don't think so,' he drawled. 'I'd better take you with me.'

Tammy jumped. 'I'll close the gates,' she said eagerly, too eagerly.

This produced his unpleasant smile, his eyes glinted at her. 'I see you have as much inclination for my company as I have for yours,' he said harshly. 'But I'm not letting you loose on my property without an escort. Do you ride?' he barked at her.

'No,' said Tammy, hoping that would be an end to it.

His lips curled. 'Real little city type, aren't you?' he jeered. 'You know, you didn't come very well equipped to snare your rich rancher, did you?'

Tammy remained silent. Rick made an impatient movement.

97

'I'll have you taught,' he said.

'No, thank you,' said Tammy quickly. 'I—I'm afraid of horses. It wouldn't be worth it anyway,' she looked beyond him carefully studying the cool white ceiling. 'I don't intend to stay here longer than the two years I've signed for.'

He gave her a sardonic look. 'Still marking the days off on your calendar?' he said softly.

Tammy flushed. He didn't miss much, she thought.

'I shouldn't,' he drawled, 'put too much hope on the ending of the assignment. Who knows? By that time I may decide you're much too valuable a help to lose.'

That, thought Tammy despairingly, was exactly what he would do if given the chance. She would still be his secretary with grey hair tied up in a bun. She shuddered.

He gave a low laugh. Tammy had a feeling he knew what she had been thinking.

'Get your hat,' he said curtly, then pointed to her lunch pack. 'You won't need that.'

As Tammy returned to the kitchen and replaced the food in the frigidaire, then went back to her room to collect her hat, she wondered when there would be an end to this persecution. This should have been her weekend off. It was in her contract, she got weekends off. She banged the straw hat on her head and reluctantly went out of the homestead. Rick was standing by the utility, his fingers impatiently tapping the bonnet. He stared, then frowned. 'We're not attending a garden party. Is that all you have in the way of a hat?' he demanded.

'What's wrong with it?' Tammy asked belligerently.

'Everything,' he replied curtly. 'Well, let's see what the stores have got.'

Tammy watched him stride off. She took off her hat and gazed at it. It was a lovely hat, she had particularly liked the large blue bow at the back. She was brought back from her musings by an impatient, 'Are you coming?' and looked up to see him standing scowling at her.

There was no shortage of hats in the stores, the only difficulty was the size. Rick banged hat after hat on her head, only to see them slip down slowly over her ears. Tammy felt like a tailor's dummy. In exasperation he finally settled on one that just stopped by her ears. 'That will have to do,' he said brusquely. 'Come on, we've wasted enough time as it is.'

Tammy followed him out, and the movement made the hat slip even further down. She turned the brim up. When they got back to the car, Rick took one look at her and commanded, 'Turn that brim down, the idea is to keep the sun off you.'

She obligingly did so. 'Thing is,' she muttered, lost under the hat completely, 'I like to see where I'm going.'

'For heaven's sake!' he shouted, then gave an explosive, 'Okay, wear that damned straw. Give the storekeeper your hat size on Monday. Got it? Now get in.'

Tammy did so, feeling ridiculously pleased with her little success over the hat. She hadn't taken to the store hats at all.

CHAPTER EIGHT

THEY drove past the paddocks and out of the homestead grounds. Soon they were passing acres and acres of pasture land Tammy could see no sheep, and longed to ask why this was so. She remembered reading somewhere that sheep did not thrive in tropical climates. perhaps they were much higher up in the distant hills she could only just see on the horizon. She glanced at the grim countenance of the man beside her, but he did not look in the mood to enlighten her, so she sighed inwardly and gave her attention once more to the passing scenery. It seemed they had been driving for miles before they came to any sign of habitation. She saw a small homestead in the distance and it soon became obvious that Rick Hatton was heading for it. Suddenly a gate appeared before them.

'That,' he said, 'is a gate.'

Tammy bristled. She could see it was a gate!

'Well,' he went on, slowing up as they came to it, 'get out and open it, and close it when I'm through,' he ordered.

How, she asked herself, could one love a man like that? She must have had a touch of the sun when she imagined she did. She loathed him—nevertheless, she did as she was told.

No luxury fittings here, thought Tammy, as they drove up the dirt track to the homestead. The outbuildings were not too well looked after, in fact it appeared to her that a strong gale might well blow the lot down. As the car drew up in front of the homestead the screened door opened and a faded-looking woman stood on the front step. 'Day, Rick,' she called, and came to meet them.

'Day, Jean,' he answered. 'How's Dan?' The question was asked mildly, almost, thought Tammy in some surprise, kindly. He got out. Tammy felt the woman glance at her curiously before she answered.

'Going on fine, thanks, Rick. He's looking forward to your visit.'

Rick Hatton turned to Tammy. 'There's some magazines in the back, get them.'

No please or thank you, thought Tammy. She found them and took them to him, handing them to him as he stood talking to the woman. Then he turned and went into the homestead.

The woman called Jean stayed. She gave Tammy a nervous smile. Tammy realised she would have to make the introductions—he really was the limit!

'Er—secretary. Tammy Dainton,' she said, holding out her hand.

Taking it, the woman exclaimed, 'Say, you're the English girl, then. We heard he'd got a secretary.'

As long, thought Tammy darkly, as that was all they had heard. She smiled. 'Your husband sick?' she asked.

The woman nodded. 'Crocked his back six months ago. Doc thinks he'll make out, but it'll be a long pull.' She nodded back towards the homestead. 'Any other boss,' she said, 'would have sent us packing, but not Rick Hatton. One of the best, he is, comes every week just like today and brings magazines for him to look at.'

A fair slight young girl appeared round the corner of the homestead; she wore jeans and checked shirt. She gave Tammy a sharp questioning look as she moved towards them.

'My daughter Mandy,' said the woman. 'Mandy, come and say hallo to . . .' She looked apologetically at Tammy. 'I forgot . . .'

'Tammy,' supplied Tammy.

'Miss Tammy,' the woman introduced.

The girl appeared uninterested and managed just to get out, 'Hallo', then walked on past them into the homestead.

Her mother, staring after her, turned back to Tammy. 'Take no notice,' she said. 'Calf love. She was hoping Rick would take her over to the settlements, that's his next stop. Sometimes he takes her with him, drops her off on his way back. She's just plain jealous, that's all.'

'Jealous?' echoed Tammy, eyebrows raised.

The woman chuckled. 'You haven't worked for Rick long, that's plain to see. You'll find every woman under thirty will be out for your blood. Especially if he's including you in these trips. Met Miss Scott yet?' she asked with a twinkle in her eye.

Tammy shook her head.

'You will,' promised the woman. 'But watch out for her claws. If she thinks you're after her property she'll skin you alive.' She chuckled. 'I'd kinda like to see her face when she finds out he's carting you around on these trips.' She looked out at the plains stretching into the distance and nodded. 'I'd like to see that madam come unstuck.'

'Are they engaged?' asked Tammy, thinking that for an engaged man Rick was certainly free with his embraces.

'Well, depends on what way you look at it,' the woman said slowly. 'From her way, yes. From Rick's, I doubt it. Nothing official, as you might say—still,' she sighed, 'you never know. Her family ranks pretty high in society around here and from that point of view it would be a suitable match. He might give a pretty girl a whirl, but he'd be pretty choosey when it came to marriage—he's a proud man.'

Tammy was all too aware of this fact. The subject of their conversation then strode out of the homestead. He nodded to the woman and got into the car. Tammy smiled her goodbye and hastily got in too.

As the car moved off, Tammy wondered why he hadn't brought Mandy with him. She was a little sorry; at least she would have had someone to talk to.

After several more gates, which Tammy, needing no more bidding, got out and opened, they came to the settlements. Rough wooden shacks grouped together and the smell of wood fires was Tammy's first impression of the aborigine settlement. A bunch of small children who appeared to share one suit between two of them, the shirt on one and the trousers on another, clustered around the car as it stopped, Not one tiny dark hand touched the bonnet. They were obviously well drilled in the correct distance to keep from the boss man's property. Rick Hatton got out. This time he did not ask Tammy to look for what was wanted, but rummaged in the back himself, emerging with several packets. A very large stout aboriginal woman whose dress made Tammy blink—she wouldn't have thought it possible to combine so many colours on one strip of material—came waddling towards them. Her white teeth flashed as she called, 'Day, Boss, Boyo's out on track.'

Rick Hatton returned the greeting. 'Day, Tess. Can't stop this time, running late. See these get distributed, will you?' He got back into the car, before he started up he looked at the tallest of the group of children. 'Parcel with blue string, William, fair shares for everyone—okay?'

The way the child's face lit up made Tammy desperately wish she could like Rick Hatton. That she was in a minority was clear. He was tops as far as his people went. She gazed out at the rolling plains as they set off again. Bleakly she thought, she had not been given much chance to like him, all because of what had happened in the past. She gave him a sideways look. He now wore a stetson as the heat was beginning to penetrate. Under its partial shade he looked even more forbidding. How old was he? She wondered. Not much more than thirty, she surmised. Well, in that case he would have been about eight years old when it happened. She felt the sharp prick behind her eyes. To think she had had to land up on his doorstep of all people's, in a place as large as Australia!

His curt voice broke in on her thoughts. 'The next place is old Josh's. He's a bit of a recluse, has no time for women. You can stretch your legs if you want to, but keep away from the homestead. Got that?'

Tammy nodded.

The homestead they drew up in front of was very dilapidated. Old bits of machinery scattered the surrounding yards, and what might have once been called curtains flapped out of grimy windows. An old rocking chair sat on the verandah. The sun was well up and Tammy felt the heat. She decided she would get out, if only to get a little breeze if there was any going.

She watched Rick Hatton stride off into the homestead, and stood looking around her. The green pastures had long since vanished. Here was only sparse greenery dotted amongst dust tracks. The yard she was standing in was mostly made up of dry sandy soil. She wondered whether in days gone by this had been a thriving cattle station—the rotting old sheds seemed to hint at such a past. Perhaps the lack of water had doomed it years ago. What must have once been a paddock was now nothing but a bare space with odd tufts of greenery sprouting out at intervals over the area. The fence had long since ceased to function as such, and what was left of the stumps could still be seen protruding out of the barren ground. Tammy sighed. It was very depressing. She could almost sense the heartbreak of what had once been. Someone had once called this home she thought.

She became aware of a slight movement near a bush beyond one of the stumps. She looked again. Yes, there it was again—a slight rustling. She continued watching. A slim almost emaciated form of a dog emerged and stood uncertainly watching her. There was something wrong with its right foreleg. It limped a little nearer, then whined piteously. Tammy took a step towards it, but was pulled up by a sharp command.

'Leave it—unless you want to get torn to pieces. Get back into the car.' Tammy stared at Rick Hatton, who stood on the verandah steps with an old man who to Tammy's wondering eyes looked like Rip van Winkle. White hair seemed to sprout out from all angles of his head and face. His weatherbeaten face was almost totally eclipsed by side whiskers. In spite of the heat he wore an ancient leather waistcoat, his dilapidated trousers were tied at the knees by string.

She looked back at Rick Hatton, who watched her with narrowed eyes. She realised she would have to obey him and got back into the car. He walked towards the dog. 'Scat!' he said menacingly. 'Home, Janty.'

Tammy watched the dog crouch for a second or so, then painfully hobble away. She bit her lip. She saw Rick Hatton walk away in the direction of the sheds with the old-timer.

In a very short while she saw the dog again. It was back again near the bush. She watched it crouch down and lay the injured leg out, awkwardly exposing the pads of the paw. So that was it! Stone or thorn whatever it was, that poor thing was asking as plainly as if it spoke for help.

Tammy glanced back to where Rick Hatton and the old man had gone, but there was no sign of them. She got out of the car and made her way towards the injured animal. As she got closer she saw the amber eyes watch her every move, but it stayed put. It can't be wild, thought Tammy, it had enough sense to seek help from humans. Besides, Rick Hatton had called it by name. What had he called it? Janty. That was it. Softly murmuring the name, Tammy got down on all fours and slowly crawled nearer the animal.

She did not go directly to the injured paw, but first stroked the soft muzzle of the dog. The eyes still continued their watchful wait. Then without turning her back she edged slowly back to where the paw lay exposed. Sure enough the trouble lay deeply embedded in the soft pad of the paw. It was a wicked-looking black thorn. The area where it had pierced through was swollen, and Tammy could guess the pain the animal was in. Gently she eased the thorn out. The dog whimpered now and again. After what seemed like ages, she had the long black spike in the palm of her hand.

'There now,' she said. 'Clean it up, boy.' She started to get up and found her wrist caught in an iron grip and she was swung on her feet with a force that took her breath away.

Her gasp of surprise was stilled when she met the blazing eyes of Rick Hatton. He looked as if he would murder her on the spot—Tammy flinched back from the fury of those eyes. He caught hold of her shoulders in a grip of steel and shook her as if she had been a rag doll; he wasn't content with shaking her until her head and neck ached, he shouted at her as well—a furious tirade that Tammy couldn't possibly attend to, all she knew was he was hurting her. His fingers dug into her shoulder bones and she vaguely wondered whether he was trying to break her neck.

When he eventually released her she was aching all over; she stood trying to catch her breath, and heard the old-timer mutter, 'Easy there now, Rick, she's had enough.'

'Stay out of this, Josh,' grated Rick Hatton, 'You know as well as I do, first rule of the bush is to learn to take orders and obey them, and by heaven, she'll learn!'

Tammy stood swaying a little. He really had hurt. Her blazing eyes met his implacable grey ones. More than her pride was stinging from this latest and most uncalled-for attack. Rick just stood and looked at her. Tammy put all her five foot two into the swinging slap at the man who had caused her such indignity. Two things registered on her consciousness, the surprised expression on Rick Hatton's face as he took the slap, and the grin on the old-timer's face—she noted absently how his mouth seemed to disappear into his whiskers.

Tammy stood defiantly facing Rick Hatton, daring him to touch her again. She saw the move he made towards her, and the sudden check, the hands clench, and the furiously working muscle at the side of his mouth. Then she found herself swung over his shoulder and carried like a sack of potatoes to the car. He all but threw her in.

'If you know what's good for you, you'll stay put till I'm ready!' he grated out.

With smouldering eyes Tammy watched him go back into the homestead. She blinked hard, but was unable to stop the tears that welled up. Of all the hateful men she had to come up against, she had to pick a boss like that! He never missed a chance to take it out on her. She rubbed a small and now rather grubby fist against her eyes to wipe away the tears. Suddenly she felt a hand on her shoulder and jumped, not only with surprise, for she was extremely sore there. It was the old-timer Josh. His gnarled old hand patted her.

'Fine thing yer did there, missy,' he mumbled out of his whiskers, 'even if yer did get a shaking fer it. Guess yer pretty mad at Rick, ain't yer?'

Tammy gulped but said nothing; mad wasn't the

word!

He nodded, then mumbled, 'Yer 'ang on a mo, git yer a drink,' and was gone.

He came back a short time later holding an ancient mug. Tammy looked doubtfully at it. She didn't like to refuse and it did smell good. It was coffee. She took it, and smiled her thanks out of tear-misted eyes.

Josh jerked his head back at the homestead. 'Rick's on the radio, just checking up on the outstations.' He then produced a rather bedraggled-looking gentian-coloured flower, not dissimilar to a pansy, which he shyly presented to Tammy.

'Kinda the same colour of yer eyes,' he mumbled.

It was too much for Tammy, and she felt the tears spill over as she gratefully thanked him. He stood and shuffled his feet in the dust for a second or so. Tammy sipped her coffee. It was strong. She coughed as the liquid slipped down her throat. 'Josh, what's in it?' she spluttered.

Again that grin that hid his mouth. 'Thought yer needed a pick-up. There's good brandy in that, missy.' Tammy sipped more slowly, very concious of the honour that had been given her. The old-timer wouldn't have too much of that to splash about.

'Yer—' he began again. 'Guess yer still pretty mad. Rick don't give no walloping for nothin, yer know,' It was, felt Tammy, a debatable point where she was concerned. However, she gravely listened to Josh.

'I never seed Rick scared afore, but he were mighty scared when he catched yer taking that there thorn out. White as a sheet he was. Guess that was what the walloping was fer—making 'im scared, I mean. Mind yer, stands to reason if dog was going to attack yer, 'e'd never 'ad let yer git near 'im. Told Rick so, but 'e was mad as fire 'e 'adn't got 'is gun. Just as well, ole Janty wouldn't 'ave thought much of 'aving 'is dog shot.'

'Why didn't old Janty—I mean Mr Janty take the thorn out himself, then,' said Tammy indignantly. 'It must have been in there for days.'

Old Josh scratched his whiskers where Tammy presumed his chin lay. ' 'E'd be up in hills, I guess. No one else can 'andle the dog, see. I wouldn't 'ave tried, nor Rick. Guess yer got a way with dogs.'

Tammy explained. 'Dad was a vet,' she said. 'I used to help him. You see, Josh, animals know when you want to help them.'

Josh nodded solemnly, then glanced up at the homestead, and Tammy followed his glance. Rick Hatton had just emerged. Tammy's lips tightened. She thanked Josh for the drink and handed him the empty mug, his flower she cradled on her lap.

Rick Hatton got in the car; he didn't even give Tammy a glance. He nodded to Josh, 'Day, Josh,' and started up.

As the car swung back on the outward track Josh shouted, 'Bring Missie again, Rick!'

Rick Hatton's expression was grim and he did not reply.

They drove for several miles in studied silence.

Several times the car would bump over uneven terrain, and Tammy felt every rut they ran into. She winced and gingerly felt the back of her neck. Rick must have been watching her as he had a grin on his face as he enquired politely, 'Sore?'

Tammy refrained from answering this provocative question. She kept her head averted after that, and stared out at the passing landscape. Next weekend, she vowed, she would be off at sun-up. She was not risking an outing like this again.

'If it's any consolation,' he murmured, 'you pack quite a wallop.' He thoughtfully fingered his right cheek.

'Good!' said Tammy in heartfelt tones.

He threw back his head and laughed. 'You know, Miss Dainton, you're a very refreshing person. It's a pity you're not in my league, I might otherwise be tempted to give you quite a run for your money.'

'From my point of view,' ground out Tammy, 'it's a thanksgiving occasion. I'd prefer old Josh,' and she touched the petals of the flower.

He glanced down at it. 'Did he give you that? Well, well. Sorry for you, was he?'

The car ran over another rut. Tammy grimaced. She did wonder if he was doing it deliberately.

'He sympathised, more like,' said Tammy scathingly. 'In his way he was trying to make up for the rough treatment I'd received.'

Rick Hatton's jaw squared, his eyes narrowed. 'One of these days, Miss Dainton, I'll throttle you,' he said softly. 'You know darn well why you got that shaking. That dog's known to be vicious, you could have got torn to pieces. And I did warn you. Perhaps you'll listen to what I tell you next time, or so help me I'll put you over my knee and really wallop you, no matter who's around—understand?'

Tammy saw no point in answering. She looked out again. The scenery they were now passing had reverted back to green pastures, and cattle could be seen grazing in the distance.

'The next stop is the Scotts' place,' he said curtly. 'We shall be invited to lunch and probably supper.' He glanced at Tammy. 'Get some of that dust off you,' he ordered. 'You're carrying half of Josh's yard around with you.'

Tammy stared at him. Scott—wasn't that the name of the girl who was probably going to marry him? Well, she could do without meeting that kind of high society.

'Drop me off,' she said. 'I'm not in the mood for company.'

Rick jammed his foot down on the brake causing Tammy more discomfiture. She glared at him.

He sat and looked at her. 'What do you intend to do?' he drawled. 'Walk the fifteen miles back?'

'Just point me in the right direction,' said Tammy obstinately. 'You can pick me up on the way back if I'm still walking.'

'I'll do no such thing!' he shouted at her. 'You're coming with me, and that's an end to it.' He gave her

114

a hard look. 'What in tarnation have you done to your face? Looks as if you've got a beaut of a black eye. Are you going to get cleaned up? Or am I going to clap your face in one of the troughs?'

'I don't see,' ground out Tammy, 'what difference it makes whether they see me with a black eye or not. They might as well know now just how I'm treated. There must be a society for the protection of secretaries from bullying bosses somewhere,' she ended plaintively.

He looked straight ahead, then to Tammy's disgust his shoulders started shaking. 'You'll have to start a branch of Women's Lib,' he managed to get out.

'Very funny,' replied Tammy icily.

He gave her an amused look and dived into a side pocket of the car and produced a small but dainty mirror. Tammy stared at it. It was a woman's property. She could guess who owned it.

He handed it to her. 'Kept,' he murmured, 'for emergency purposes.'

Tammy's expression showed what she thought of that. She held it gingerly and looked at the dust marks on her face. She couldn't see how, without a handkerchief or water, she could do anything about it, and said as much.

He sighed elaborately and produced his handkerchief. It was spotless. It was a shame to use it, thought Tammy. Then he produced a small water bottle and sprinkled the water liberally on to the white linen, then handed it to her silently with a look that said,

'Any more excuses?'

The Scotts' homestead was not as big as Wamoshanta and the surrounding grounds, although neat and well looked after, had not the lush vegetation or lovely herbaceous bushes that nestled around Wamoshanta. It was as if, thought Tammy, an effort had been made to keep up appearances, but it was a race against time. They might be high society, but they were nowhere near the financial bracket of Rick Hatton.

As before, the door of the homestead was open before the car drew up. Rick Hatton climbed out. Tammy stared at the girl posing—you couldn't call it anything else, she thought—on the verandah steps. It was the redhead Mrs Morris had told her about, and Tammy had to admit she was beautiful. Her voluptuous figure was tightly enclosed in a pale blue dress that left nothing to the imagination. Her hair was long and hung about her shoulders. Yes, thought Tammy, if that was Rick's type she could well understand why he called her skinny. Her heart sank. Depression settled like a cloud about her. Josh's pick-up had worn off, leaving Tammy with her misery of bruised shoulders and the wretched situation she was in. She climbed stiffly out of the car, still clutching the little flower.

She heard the murmured, 'Darling', said in a husky voice and wondered what she ought to do if they went into a clinch. However, she was not put to the embarrassment of watching any such reunion. Rick Hatton briefly touched the redhead on the shoulder nd then turned to Tammy.

'Diana, meet Miss Dainton—secretary, proving in-
aluable,' he said, baiting Tammy once more. 'Miss
Dainton, this is Diana Scott, an old friend.'

Diana's eyebrows went up at the 'old friend' bit,
ut she recovered swiftly and held a well manicured
and out to Tammy. Taking it and noting how long
er red nails were, Tammy remembered the woman's
emarks about her, and almost shuddered. She had,
hought Tammy, built-in tools for the 'tear you to
ieces' remark.

'You're English, aren't you, Miss Dainton?' queried
he girl.

Tammy nodded, noting how the smile she gave her
id not reach those green eyes of hers. She doesn't like
ne, thought Tammy. As she answered, she wondered
vhat on earth she was doing there, miles away from
ome, a complete alien and forced to endure the
ompany of a man, and here a woman, who quite
efinitely disliked her.

She followed them miserably into the homestead.
A stout man bustled towards them as they entered.

'Rick, come in. Nice to see you. Hallo, who have
ve here?' His bright blue eyes rested on Tammy.

Introductions were made again. The man was
Diana's father. 'Mother will be out in a minute.
he's making sure Trudy doesn't burn the meringues,'
ie said. 'Come along, I don't know why we're all
tanding here,' and he took Tammy's arm and led her
nto a room off the hall. It was large and airy, what

Tammy would have called a sitting room, several occasional tables and a large walnut sideboard or which stood some china ornaments and a huge vase of flowers. It was a beautiful arrangement. Tammy's eyes rested on it.

Mr Scott, who settled himself beside her, remarked 'Mother's hobby—made a good job of that, hasn't she?'

Tammy nodded. 'It's quite an art, isn't it? I'm afraid I just dump them in and hope for the best.' With a start she noticed she was still holding Josh's flower. 'Do you think I might beg some water for this little one?' she asked.

'Sure thing,' replied Mr Scott. 'Come on out and meet the wife, she's in the kitchen.'

Tammy followed him, aware of Rick Hatton's eyes on her as he listened to whatever it was Diana was telling him in her husky voice.

Mrs Scott was a woman of large proportions also; Tammy could see where Diana got her curves from, and couldn't help wondering a little naughtily whether she would in later years overflow to the extent that her mother had, but she quickly banished these unworthy thoughts, as she took the hand Mrs Scott held out to her with an open smile. As Tammy stood talking to them in the spotless kitchen she wished she could stay there for the rest of the time to be spent with the Scotts. At least she was out of hearing and sight of Rick Hatton. It was a relief to be out of his presence.

CHAPTER NINE

LUNCH was served in the dining room. Tammy was placed next to Mr Scott, with his wife on her other side. Rick Hatton sat with Diana opposite him. This arrangement suited Tammy. To speak to her Rick would have to lean over Mrs Scott, so she was not likely to be troubled by him during lunch at least.

Tammy really enjoyed the meal. It was a salad and most welcome after the heat of the morning. She hadn't realised she was so hungry. There was a good assortment of cooked meats to go with it, and Tammy chose cold chicken. She noticed how Diana Scott kept up a constant flow of small talk directed only at Rick Hatton; considering the company, it was a little bad-mannered, but Tammy was not complaining, she was only too relieved to have his attention taken from her.

'Are you any relation of Celia Dainton? They run racing stables at Newbury?' queried Mrs Scott, as she handed Tammy a dish of fresh baked bread rolls.

'Gracious me, no,' said Tammy hastily. 'I come from just an ordinary family, you know. I'm what you might call a nobody of a typist from England.' She could not resist that one. She knew Rick Hatton had caught the remark by the way his lips straightened as he leaned forward to take a bread roll.

Mr Scott laughed, then said, 'What's your fir[s]t name? We can't go on calling you Miss Dainton, it[']s so formal.'

Tammy was about to reply when Rick Hatto[n] spoke.

'It's Delilah,' he murmured. 'I rather think it sui[ts] her, don't you?'

Tammy was about to refute this when the sad fac[t] struck her that if she said 'Tammy', they would b[e] sure to ask what it was short for, and she couldn'[t] bear Rick Hatton to get hold of that bit of informatio[n].

'Really?' Mr and Mrs Scott spoke in unison.

Tammy nodded. She noted with pleasure the star[e] Rick Hatton gave at this assent.

'How strange,' murmured Mrs Scott, then realise[d] this was not a very complimentary remark and sai[d] hurriedly, 'Well, I think it's a lovely name.'

Tammy nodded gravely. 'It's a family name,' sh[e] added.

Rick Hatton made a strangled noise as he choke[d] over a piece of bread roll.

When lunch was over, Diana suggested they g[o] riding. For politeness' sake she had to include Tamm[y] in her invitation, but Tammy was only too pleased t[o] inform her that she did not ride.

'I'm having her taught,' said Rick Hatton with [a] gleam in his eye.

Tammy met his eyes squarely. 'Sorry,' she sai[d] firmly, 'but I'd have no use for it back home, so it'[s] just a waste.' She turned to Mr Scott. 'I'm only her[e] for a two-year period, you see, and I'm terrified of horses.'

'It's just a question of approach,' said Rick Hatton. 'You'll soon lose your fear of them.' It was quietly but determinedly said.

Tammy glared at him. If he thought for one minute he was going to make her he had another think coming!

Mr Scott looked from one to the other of them, then said, 'Shouldn't push it, Rick. Remember she's English, not like our girls, practically born in the saddle. If she wants to take it up later there's nothing to stop her.'

'She'll learn,' repeated Rick Hatton, and turned to Diana. 'Well, how about that ride?'

Before they left, he spoke softly to Tammy. 'Think you can stay out of trouble for an hour or so, Delilah?'

Tammy was still fuming about the incident of horse riding and did not bother to answer.

Mr and Mrs Scott entertained her during their absence, and Tammy noticed how Mrs Scott's manner had somewhat altered from her first openly friendly attitude. Tammy would catch her giving her occasional summing up glances. She's afraid I'm going to put a spoke in Diana's wheel, she thought. She doesn't know the reason Rick Hatton is paying me so much attention.

Rick Hatton and Diana returned well before the hour was up. Tammy thought Diana looked a bit sulky and caught a few smouldering glances directed at her.

They sat talking in the sitting room until supper. It was now dark and the room was lit by a solitary standard lamp in the corner of the room.

Diana spoke to her for the first time almost since her arrival. 'Do you get homesick, Delilah?' she asked.

Tammy wished she hadn't asked that question. The coming of dark, the shadows cast by the old lamp, somehow reminiscent of home, had brought that familiar lump to her throat.

'Very,' she replied quietly.

'Left anyone at home?' persisted Diana.

Tammy began to see the reasoning behind this seemingly sympathetic questioning. 'No family, if that's what you mean,' she answered, knowing full well it wasn't.

'But someone special, I mean,' probed Diana.

'I'm not engaged, or anything like that,' replied Tammy, wishing the subject could be changed. She could feel Rick Hatton's eyes on her even if she couldn't see his expression.

Diana's voice was non-committal as she replied, 'Oh, I just wondered, that's all. Only you seem anxious, as it were, to get back.'

'It's natural she would be homesick,' cut in Mr Scott. 'No place like home, I say.' He patted Tammy's knee. 'It gets easier as time goes by. I know, I'm from the Old Country myself. Mind you, it's some years now, but I know how I felt. Almost chucked it in several times, and took the first boat home. Glad I didn't now, of course.'

'You see, Delilah,' said Rick Hatton softly, 'it's just a question of time.'

Only Tammy knew the meaning behind those deceptively soft words and she felt the tears threatening again to spill over. As if she didn't feel bad enough. She was tired, sore, and homesick, and couldn't wait to get back to Wamoshanta to weep it out of her system.

They were off directly after supper. Tammy went ahead quickly and got into the utility. She didn't intend to embarrass either Rick Hatton or Diana by witnessing their goodnight kiss. But to her surprise Rick Hatton was right behind her. Diana walked with him to the car. Tammy saw her raise her face for the expected kiss, only to receive the same careless pat on the shoulder. She heard the half exasperated 'Rick!' and his cool 'Night, Di', as he got into the car.

In all probability, mused Tammy, they had exchanged the passionate clinches when they were out riding. She felt her cheeks grow hot. Rick Hatton would be no half-hearted lover. All the same, it was odd, you'd think he could have managed a quick kiss for Diana, she thought.

Tammy fell asleep on the return journey, and Rick Hatton seemed indisposed for conversation. She felt a light touch on her shoulder, and blinked into the surrounding darkness. 'We're home,' he said curtly.

Tammy climbed out, forgetting her aches and pains

for a second, then the stiffness reminded her and she almost groaned.

'Pack an overnight bag,' he ordered as she walked stiffly into the homestead.

'I beg your pardon,' said Tammy sleepily, not yet properly awake.

'Snap out of it!' he barked. 'Are you listening to me?'

'Yes,' yawned Tammy.

'Well, go and pack, then. You may have forgotten it, but Mrs Morris is away. Now do you get it?'

Tammy blinked and tried hard to concentrate. 'What,' she murmured, 'has that to do with it?'

He stood studying her silently. 'I don't think you've quite worked out the implications, so I'll help you.' His eyes then narrowed. 'Or perhaps you have,' he murmured. 'Well, you might trust me, Delilah, but I don't trust you.'

Tammy made an effort to follow his line of reasoning. What on earth was he meandering on about? Something about not trusting her.

'I don't intend becoming your rich rancher, Delilah, and have no intentions of being coerced into what's called a compromising situation.'

Tammy stood blinking at him. The message finally got through. 'Compromising situation. Don't intend becoming your rich rancher . . .' Slowly it all registered in Tammy's tired brain. She closed her eyes. It really was the last straw! She went white, and abruptly turned away and went straight to her room, collected

her night things and put them in a small case, returning to Rick Hatton who was standing by the front
door where she had left him.

She got into the car and sat with averted face, her
features stiff.

Starting up the car, he remarked, 'I'm taking you
to Mr Hampton's for the night.'

Tammy didn't answer—she couldn't. She could feel
the tears lining up again. She clenched her teeth; she
would not cry in front of this man.

When they got to Wamanta, there was a light on in
the porch. They were expected, apparently. Rick
Hatton must have phoned through, she thought
wearily.

'Have a hot bath,' he ordered when they got out,
'it will help ease the soreness.'

Tammy didn't answer.

'Do you hear me?' he demanded.

Tammy remained silent.

'Have it your way, then,' he grated. 'I'm collecting
you at eleven.'

This time Tammy did speak. She whirled round.
'Don't bother,' she managed to get out. 'I want and
need this weekend off in . . . in . . .' Her voice faltered,
to her horror she felt the tears spill over. She rushed
into the house.

Paula was waiting up for her. 'Tammy, what's the
matter?' she cried. 'Have you had another row with
Rick?'

Wiping the tears away, Tammy replied, 'I'm homesick, Paula, that's all. Be a pet and let me have a good cry.'

Paula patted her on the arm. 'Okay, Tammy, see you in the morning.'

CHAPTER TEN

AT breakfast next morning Tammy's eyelids were heavy and her manner despondent. Paula tried to cheer her up by suggesting she join her and some friends at tennis later that morning. Tammy thanked her, but refused. Mr Hampton reminded Paula that Tammy couldn't go anyway as Rick was calling for her at eleven. Not that Tammy needed any reminding. During her almost sleepless night one thing she had promised herself, and that was one day out of sight and sound of Rick Hatton. By hook or by crook she was going to have that day. Gerry was having a weekend off and had gone home to Queensland. Tammy was somewhat relieved about this; it might have added to the already complicated situation, had he been around.

Paula was off soon after breakfast, reminding Tammy of her promise to come to the dance next Saturday. 'We'll see,' said Tammy.

Mr Hampton was in no hurry to be off himself, and Tammy guessed he wanted to talk to her.

He gave her a quick look under his bushy eyebrows. 'How's it going, girl?' he asked worriedly. 'If it's getting you down, it's not worth it. I didn't like the idea of you going up there to work, but there wasn't much I could do about it. No use arguing with Rick, he knows what he wants and always gets it. With some folk I guess that's a bad thing, but with him . . .' He laid his coffee cup down and leant towards Tammy. 'He's a fair man, Tammy, known him since he was knee-high to a grasshopper, and anyone around here will tell the same.' He looked away, 'Still, there's no denying he's got a bug about you, girl.' He got up impatiently and paced to the window and stood looking out. 'Look, Tammy, would you like me to have a go at him? Job or no job, someone's got to do it, and I kinda feel responsible for you.'

Tammy smiled at him. Nothing would alter Rick Hatton's mind about her. As far as he was concerned she was a no-good gold-digger. So far she was the only one involved; she didn't see why Mr Hampton should lose his job all for nothing. No matter what, Rick Hatton would do just what he said he would do, keep her until her time was up, and even longer if it pleased him to do so.

She thanked him and set about putting his mind at rest. 'It's mostly homesickness, you know,' she smiled, 'and there's no cure for that. I'm not ill-treated. In fact I think in a way he's making sure I'm kept busy to keep my mind occupied. He took me on a tour of the outback stations yesterday.'

Mr Hampton's relief practically oozed from him. 'Did he?' He grinned. 'Well, well, that's a feather in your cap, young lady.'

Tammy looked at him. If only he knew! Rick

Hatton only took her because he didn't trust her loose on his property.

'Rick makes a point of doing those trips solo. Oh, sometimes he picks up a passenger and drops them off, en route as it were, but taking them on the whole trip—well now, that's something. Why, even Miss Scott hasn't been afforded that honour, and she angled for it often enough.' He grinned again. 'Means a whole day in his company, you see? Well, well.'

Tammy got worried. Rick Hatton would have a fit if he thought she'd boasted about the trip. 'He only took me because he didn't want me running about loose on the ranch, Mr Hampton. I guess he was kind of stuck with me, if you know what I mean.' She looked at him; suddenly she had an idea. 'It's awkward at weekends, you know,' she said. 'Do you think I could come and stay with you?' she asked.

He nodded. 'I hadn't thought of that. You know you're welcome any time, Tammy. Paula could do with your company too. No need to make any special arrangements—you just come.'

Tammy was relieved. That was one hurdle over. 'Would you mention it to Mr Hatton, please?' she asked.

'As good as done,' Mr Hampton said happily. 'Well, I suppose I ought to meander down to the paddocks and see what wants doing. Want to come?'

Tammy hastily refused. She had her own plans for the day.

After he had gone she went back into her room

and tidied it. She picked up her hat, then the sound of a car in the drive made her hastily drop it and rush to the window. It couldn't possibly be Rick! It was only ten o'clock. When she saw it was the cream van she sighed with relief and knew an urgent sense to get going. Rick might just possibly come early. She all but ran out of the homestead. She avoided going past the paddocks, but skirted round them, keeping close to the main driveway. Determined to have that walk she had been cheated out of yesterday, she followed the long drive out of the homestead.

It was cool and refreshing in the open air. Tammy glanced up at the brilliant blue azure sky. A slight breeze rustled the bushes along the driveway. Tammy wished she had remembered to collect some food. She intended to be out for as long as the light held.

Now that she was out of the driveway, she stood looking around her. Which way? She caught sight of blossoms, pink and white in the distance. Orchards, she presumed, and decided it would be lovely to wander among the blossom-laden trees. She did not realise that distance in the summer haze was deceptive.

She passed through a pine forest that reminded her of home, and as she walked over the pine-needled ground, she thought of Rick Hatton and his uncomplimentary remarks of the previous evening. If it were not for Jonathan, she would feel the most unloved person in the world. So she had not got Diana's curves, never would have, but that was no reason for Rick Hatton to make her feel like the ugly duckling, quite apart from his insulting innuendoes about her motives for coming to Australia. She stood for a moment and watched the beams of the sun break through a deeply shadowed area of the forest. She inhaled the pine scented air and thought sadly how wonderful everything would be were it not for one insufferable male who had a liking for his own way.

Walking out of the forest, she blinked in the strong sunlight and felt the heat on her head. She had forgotten her hat! Of all the stupid things to do! What now? Peering around her, she looked for more shady spots to wander in, and groaned inwardly; there was absolutely no shade apart from the pine forest she had just come through. Either she went back and spent the rest of the day with that Napoleonic character— or she risked it. Glancing at her watch and seeing it was just past eleven decided her. If she went back, she wouldn't arrive until eleven-thirty at the earliest, and the very thought of meeting the fuming Rick Hatton was decidedly off putting.

Having made the decision, she walked on, conscious of the fact that the sun's rays were getting stronger as time passed.

If it had not been for the voice she would have walked past the high fenced area bordered with creepers. It was a male voice and the strains of 'Onward Christian Soldiers' came floating towards her. Tammy followed the well-worn track until she came to a white-painted gate, not unlike an English lychgate. Opening it and passing down a narrow path, she

came upon a small building solidly built of brick.
Coming to the heavy doors, she realised with a small
spurt of pleasure it was a chapel. The doors were open
and Tammy stepped gratefully into the cool interior.
The rough-hewn pews were empty, and she sat down
in the end row and looked about her.

It was plain but beautiful, the only ornamentation
was on the altar, a brilliantly embroidered altar-cloth.
On it stood a lovely old wooden cross flanked on either
side by flowers lovingly arranged.

As Tammy sat enveloped in the peace, she watched
a shaft of light pierce down from the only stained glass
window. It shot across the aisle in a myriad dancing
colours. If only, she felt, one could hold the peace that
pervaded the very atmosphere around here, problems
would simply cease to exist. She sighed.

'Day. Can I help you?' murmured a mild voice
behind her.

Tammy turned and met the quizzical blue eyes of
a small man. Instinctively she knew this was the
pastor. There was nothing in his apparel to suggest
this, however; he wore an old checked shirt, much
faded after countless washings and denims more or
less in the same condition. Large old gardening boots
were on his feet, and in his hand he held a small
trowel. 'No service, I'm afraid, until this evening,' he
added.

Tammy smiled at him. She wondered whether to
return his native greeting, but stuck to the English
one. 'Good morning. I'm afraid I'm only a refugee

from the sun. I forgot to take a hat when I left this morning.'

The blue eyes twinkled at her. 'And not only from the sun. Been out here long?'

Tammy told him. She also told him she was working there.

'You must be the English girl working for Rick Hatton, then,' he said, placing the trowel on the floor and carefully dusting his hands before offering one to Tammy. 'Well,' he said, after they had made the introductions, 'I've no need to ask if you're happy. He's a fine man, done a lot for the community.'

There must, thought Tammy desperately, be something radically wrong with her. Rick Hatton apparently could do wrong, but he took a delight in taunting her. Although she knew the reason, there was something personal in his very attitude to her that she was at a loss to understand. If only she could ignore him, survival would be easier, but you couldn't ignore him, at least Tammy couldn't. He could flatten her with one look.

Not wanting to keep the pastor from his garden, she was about to beg the loan of a hat of some kind when a shadow fell across the door frame. She glanced back and stiffened. Practically blocking out the sunlight was the large frame of the man himself.

'Day, Martin,' he drawled, but his eyes were on Tammy and the message they contained made her consider asking the parson for sanctuary. Tammy hastily dropped her gaze and found herself staring at something Rick Hatton held in his large well-shaped hand. Her hat! The sight of the large man holding her ridiculously inadequate straw hat did strange things to her heart, and she had to blink hastily.

'Day, Rick, nice to see you. Just been having a pow-wow with your Miss Dainton. Got time for a cup of tea?' the pastor invited.

Rick Hatton shook his head. 'Lost enough time as it is, thank you all the same, Martin.' He shot Tammy another glinting look. 'Ready?' he asked brusquely.

Tammy nodded miserably. She didn't know why she bothered. She just couldn't win. She got up slowly and walked to the door. The pastor accompanied them to the utility and invited Tammy to call any time, Tammy thanked him, but knew she would have little chance of following up the invitation.

She sat beside her stony-faced companion and waited for the blasting as they moved away from the chapel. He thrust the hat at her with a sharp 'Put it on'.

He didn't speak for some time after that and Tammy wished he would get it over with, but when he did, it was in his deceptively soft voice that Tammy dreaded, she would rather he shouted any day.

'Do you know, Delilah, I'm considered quite an expert at taming wild horses. But you're the first human variety I've tackled.' He gave her a sideways glinting look. 'But I'll tame you, my girl, if it's the last thing I do.'

'Break me, you mean,' replied Tammy dully.

He shrugged. 'Call it what you like. But you're going to learn who's boss. When I tell you to stay put you stay put. One more little demonstration like this one, and I'll really go to town on you.'

'Where it doesn't show, of course,' muttered Tammy bitterly.

He gave a low laugh. 'That's entirely up to you. There is one other way, isn't there?' he shot her a quick piercing look. 'Something else you don't like either?'

Tammy closed her eyes. She'd rather a tanning any day. 'I'd prefer a walloping,' she snapped.

He laughed again. 'And don't I know it,' he drawled softly. 'But you won't always be able to depend on that particular kind of reprisal, will you?'

'All right,' grated Tammy. 'For five days a week, I'll conform. But I am entitled to weekends off, and it's in the contract, or didn't you read that part of it? Mr Hampton said I could spend the weekends with them, and—and I shall,' she finished determinedly.

He threw her another glinting look. 'Still hankering after Gerry, Delilah?' he jeered. 'Sorry, it's not on. As for weekends off, well, that might be arranged later on, depends of course on work slackening. As my private secretary.' Tammy started and stared at him, and he grinned suddenly. 'Didn't you know that, Delilah? I rather thought Mr Selby would have explained. Didn't he mention a higher salary?'

Tammy said nothing, just stared ahead. The utility

swept up the drive of Wamoshanta and drew up in front of the homestead. Tammy made a move to get out, but Rick's hand caught her wrist.

'As I was saying,' he continued smoothly, 'as my private secretary you are, as it were, on call, no specified hours. You do know the role of a private secretary, don't you, Delilah? They travel with the boss, of course they get compensation in the high salary they receive, and yours, Delilah, is higher than most, and I don't throw my money away,' he said grimly. 'You'll be well occupied at the weekends, I'll see to that.'

Tammy had a ghastly thought. She stared at him with wide eyes. 'Not ... not learning to ride?' she almost pleaded.

He looked down at her. 'You really are afraid of horses, aren't you? What happened?' he asked abruptly.

Tammy shook her head miserably, and he made an impatient movement. 'I suppose you'll tell me when you're ready,' he said harshly. 'Like everything else it has to be dragged out of you.' He released his hold on her wrist, and climbed out of the utility.

She just sat looking ahead. He would make her ride. It would be just another way to punish her. Why hadn't she thought of these things before she came here? Everybody rode. He would not understand. Her soft lips twisted bitterly; even if he did know the reason for her fear, it would make no difference, he had no compassion where she was concerned. She closed her eyes. Jonathan was right. He said he would give her six months and she would be winging home. It was only two, and she had had enough!

'Snap out of it!' he called, bringing Tammy back with a start from her miserable musings. She got out and stood uncertainly beside him. What now? She wondered.

'Lunch,' he said abruptly. 'Then a tour of the station.'

In the kitchen Tammy eyed the food in the well-stocked fridge. There was enough there to feed a battalion. What did he like? Cold chicken? Ham, or cold beef? She shrugged. Perhaps he would help himself, but she doubted it. He had gone straight to his study. Placing a salad assortment on one dish, she placed the chicken, beef and ham on separate dishes, then went through to the dining room. She found table mats, and set the table; everything had to be searched for, this was Rick's domain and she had only barely glanced in the room since her arrival. The lovely old oak table could, she thought, seat at least twenty people. He must entertain a lot, she surmised. Odd to think of a bachelor possessing a house of this size.

As she laid the beautiful inlaid silver cutlery into place, she wondered how long ago his father had died. She also thought about the woman who had walked out on all this because she couldn't wait for the good times to come. When she had finished she gazed 'around the room. Wax polish shone on the dark furniture. The rich carpet echoed the colour of the heavy damask curtains. A large china cabinet stood on one side of the room displaying delicate exhibits behind glass. Dresden was prominent and worth a small fortune in itself. Facing the cabinet on the other side of the room was a huge carved oak sideboard on which resided a magnificent display of silver. From the ceiling hung a lovely chandelier supported by heavy gilt chains. As Tammy looked at it, the sunlight caught its gleaming drops, making them look, Tammy thought, like tears. She sighed as she turned away. It was all just a little intimidating.

'Is it the sort of thing you had in mind with your rich rancher' drawled Rick Hatton.

Tammy whirled round. How long had he stood there? She felt herself flushing, and wished she had let him get his own meal. 'No,' she said quietly, 'it's not. As a matter of fact I was just thinking it was all a bit too much.' her eyes met his squarely. 'Especially for a little nobody of a typist. I'd be completely out of my depth.'

With that she went to pass him to collect his food. He caught her arm, and looked at the table. 'You've only set for one,' he said.

'That's right,' replied Tammy. 'I'm having mine in the kitchen.'

'You will have it with me,' he said.

Again, not will you, but you will, thought Tammy. He was impossible! Her eyes gave her thoughts away.

'I wouldn't be comfortable. Thank you all the

same,' she replied, tightening her lips.

He still held her arm. 'I seem to recall someone promising to conform,' he drawled. 'Time for another lesson, Delilah?'

She stiffened. His nearness was disturbing, and she felt her heart jolt. He released her arm. 'During lunch you can tell me why you think it's,' he swung an arm around the room, 'what did you call it? A bit much?' Tammy escaped to the kitchen.

It was the most uncomfortable meal Tammy had ever had to endure. She sat opposite Rick. She would have preferred to have sat next to him, then she would not have to meet those mocking eyes each time she looked up. She had no sooner sat down than he reminded her that she had forgotten to bring the bread rolls. She began to get up when he said carelessly that it didn't matter, unless she wanted one, he rarely bothered. Tammy could have thrown something at him. Why bother to bring it up, then?

He added a few chicken slices to her plate, which further enraged her. She had quite ample for her diminished appetite.

'You know, Delilah,' he murmured, 'you've quite expressive eyes. They always give you away. They're quite lovely too—still,' his eyes narrowed, 'I expect you know all about that, they could have quite a devastating effect on an unwary male.'

Tammy swiftly looked down at her plate. Concentrate on your food, she told herself. He's only trying to rile you.

'Now tell me, what's wrong with this room?'

Tammy started. He never gave her time to collect her thoughts. She remembered not to glance up. Her eyes were on her plate as she answered slowly, 'Nothing, only its effect on people like me, brought up as it were in simple surroundings.'

'How simple?' he demanded.

Toying with her salad, she replied, 'Well, plain, then,' she answered, feeling a pang of homesickness as she thought of her old home, of the chintz-covered chairs that never stayed clean and had been the bane of Mrs Dodson their daily help's life, half the time covered with hairs and the other half spattered with muddy paws. The overflow from the surgery often landed up in their sitting room, or known fighters were hastily pushed in their to avoid mayhem in the small waiting room, and no self-respecting dog was going to sit on the floor when there were large comfortable chairs going begging.

'What was Jonathan's home like? Or didn't you get that far?'

Tammy was brought back from her musings with a jolt. She did look at him then. Of all the ...! The sparks flew from her eyes, clashing with cool grey ones.

'You declare war beautifully with your eyes,' he drawled. 'Well?'

Her lips straightened. He had asked for it! 'He has several in fact, apart from his country house, a town house, cottage on the coast, and a villa on the Riviera.'

His eyebrows rose. 'And you didn't marry him? Tut, tut, Delilah. I can't see you turning that lot down. Was he too old for you? Or did he give you a whirl and your imagination did the rest?'

Tammy resolutely declined the bait. She got up. 'Would you like some coffee?' she asked politely.

Rick didn't like that, she knew by the sudden narrowing of his eyes. However, he did not pursue the subject. 'Can you make good coffee?' he demanded.

'Of course,' said Tammy indignantly. Her father had had a thing about coffee too, and she had been well indoctrinated into the rituals.

'Very well,' he said, and rose abruptly. 'I've some paper work to finish, I'll take mine in the study.'

Later, he did acknowledge the coffee was good, which was, Tammy thought, something.

Having changed before lunch into a cool linen dress, she was somewhat surprised and not a little peeved by his sudden 'Change into slacks' order, as she was clearing the luncheon remains. She stared at him. 'For a tour of the station,' he explained carefully. 'More suitable.'

When she was ready, having only just remembered to collect her hat, she set out to find him. He was nowhere in the house. She wandered out, but still no sign of him, no sign of the utility either. Walking to the paddock fence, she leaned against the rails and stared out over the green expanses. A few minutes later she heard a sound that made her hackles rise —the steady hoof beats of a horse, and what was worse, coming behind her. It took all her will power to turn round. Rick Hatton sat astride the largest black stallion Tammy had ever seen. She cringed back against the fence as horse and rider steadily advanced.

'Meet Midnight,' he said. 'A real gentleman of a horse. He won't harm you—stroke his muzzle.'

It was all Tammy could do not to scream. This for her was a nightmare country. Her hands were tightly clenched into small fists by her side. Her back pressed into the rails of the fencing. 'No,' she managed to get out. 'Please take him away.'

She heard him give an elaborate sigh. 'On this occasion, Delilah, you can trust me. Come, make friends with him.'

Tammy could feel herself begin to shake, and turned abruptly away and held on to the fence for support. Her waist was caught and her hands wrenched from the fence, and before she realised it, he held her in front of him astride the horse. Her back was against his chest in a tight hold. 'Fear,' he murmured against her hair, 'can be overcome. Try and move with the action of the horse.'

She struggled wildly. She could see the black mane and the flaring nostrils of the stallion as he moved slowly backwards to his master's touch. For one second the hold on her was relaxed as Rick adjusted the reins, and it gave Tammy the chance to move out of that iron grip. She twisted round to throw herself off, but he caught her before she could complete the action. 'Please, no,' she whispered.

'Yes,' he said determinedly, and attempted to turn her round facing the stallion's head again.

She threw both arms around him and buried her head in his chest hanging on for dear life. 'I can't, don't you see I can't!' she cried wildly.

He let go of the reins and prised her away from him. 'If,' he said furiously, 'this is another of your feminine wiles, you're wasting your time. I firmly believe in the male making the advances, so cut it out.'

Tammy did not answer. She couldn't, she had fainted.

CHAPTER ELEVEN

AWAKING several hours later, Tammy lay looking around her. She was in her room. As her gaze slowly travelled around the familiar furniture, she tried to recall events. A drowsiness enveloped her senses, as bit by bit they came back. Her last recollections were of being cradled by someone, and being told to drink something out of a glass. It had tasted bitter; she remembered pushing the glass away, but being made to finish it. Someone had said 'Good girl'. She remembered the shaking stopping. She creased her brow. She had thought Jonathan was there, she had called his name. She sat up slowly, and shook her head. It couldn't have been Jonathan. Her gaze travelled to her arms; they were bare. Almost jerked out of her bemused state, she found she was in her nightdress, a filmy thing she had bought before she had realised the nights could become quite cold. Her cheeks grew hot. Of course it hadn't been Jonathan. Rick Hatton! He hadn't . . . Of all the . . .

The door opened and Mrs Morris walked in. 'How are you feeling?' she demanded. 'It's about time you woke.'

Tammy blinked. 'What time is it, Mrs Morris?' she asked.

'Six-thirty,' Mrs Morris replied. 'I expect you could do with a cup of tea. You just sit tight, I'll be back in a jiffy.'

Tammy couldn't bear the suspense. 'How long have you been back?' she asked quickly before Mrs Morris left the room.

Mrs Morris turned. 'Caught an earlier bus, walked in to find Mr Hatton giving you a sedative. My, my, girl, you were shaking all over! Mr Hatton said you'd had a shock of some kind. Said it was all his fault. Wouldn't rest until he'd got the doc to have a look at you.' She grinned. 'If you ask me he ought to have taken a sedative himself. Never thought I'd ever see him put out.'

Shortly after she had left, there was a tap on the door. Tammy knew it couldn't be Mrs Morris, and hastily pulled the sheet up to her chin. She could guess who it was.

Rick stood looking down at her. There was an expression on his face she had never seen before, and something about him that slightly alarmed her, of unleashed energy held in check that only a light trigger would release. He's mad again, she thought.

'Why the hell couldn't you have told me?' he demanded furiously. 'Do you think I enjoyed making you relive that again? You must have spent weeks in hospital, with those scars.'

Tammy flushed. Had he actually seen them? The ghastly thought that he must have undressed her returned again.

He noted the flush and said sardonically, 'The doctor.' He then sat down abruptly on the bed. 'What happened? The doctor said you must have been trampled to within an inch of your life.'

It was no use trying to put him off. Tammy knew that. She sighed and turned away from those searching eyes of his.

'There was a fire,' she explained, 'at a stables not far from us. Dad was called out,' she looked quickly at him, then away again. 'He was a vet,' she explained. 'Well, I went with him. We helped get the horses out, but they were quite terrified, of course. A stallion went berserk. You couldn't blame him, the place was an inferno. I shouldn't have tried to hold on to him as I brought him out.'

There was silence for a second or so, then he said, 'When are you going to trust me, Delilah?' He looked away. 'Or is it that I don't trust you?'

He got up abruptly as Mrs Morris came in with the tea tray. Before he left he said, 'I'm sending you back to Mr Hampton. Tingston is sufficiently recovered to resume his duties,' and left.

Tammy was slightly bewildered. She couldn't make head or tail of what he meant. He had spoken quite unnecessarily harshly.

Mrs Morris left the tray. She did not have time to linger, as she had the evening meal to prepare.

As she sipped her tea, and attempted to eat the thin slivers of bread, Tammy's emotions underwent a strange reversal. She should have been shouting for joy. She was going back to Mr Hampton. No more persecution, or cutting remarks. Rick was letting her go—she could sense it. Was he tired of the game? Had the novelty worn off? Her eyes filled with tears. Stop it! she scolded herself. Grow up. If you've been stupid enough to fall in love with a man that hates you, you've only yourself to blame. She remembered the way she had clung to him. Her cheeks felt hot, then a wry smile touched her lips. That must have been the last straw. He had certainly prised her away from him fast enough. How could she have thrown herself at him like that? He, of all people?

She put her cup down. The truth was, if Rick had had two heads she would have done the same thing, but he would not understand that. He must have got really worried at her fall as it were, in his arms. This thought pleased her and she began to cheer up. She was 'getting the treatment' all over again, and was being hustled back to Mr Hampton. If Rick did but know it, she thought furiously, he was quite safe from this gold-digger. Her lips straightened. He was even willing to sacrifice Gerry, apparently.

She laid the tray on the small table by the bed and got up. She would pack there and then. The very sight of her case already packed would give her morale quite a boost. She only wished she could go right away, but guessed it would be in the morning.

Tammy was picked up the following morning by Danny. She did not see Rick Hatton before she left, which pleased her; the less she saw of him the better.

Mr Hampton welcomed her back with open arms. Tammy felt it was nice to be wanted by someone. There was no sign of Gerry that evening at dinner, and while they had coffee on the verandah Mr Hampton explained the reason for his absence.

'He's been sent to the main outstation. It's sheepshearing time, and every available man is called in. Rick will be up there too for most of the week. Then at the finish, which should be this weekend, there'll be a real ding-dong of a do on Saturday night. The shearing gang come into town and Rick gives them a sort of thank-you send-off,' he grinned at Tammy. 'You'll not lack partners that night, Tammy.'

'Will Gerry be back then?' she asked.

Mr Hampton shook his head. 'Nope, he'll be away six months or more. He was due to spend another month here, but as it's shearing time Rick thought he might as well stay up there afterward.'

Tammy sipped her coffee. So he hadn't sacrificed Gerry after all, he was still protecting him, she thought bitterly.

The days went by, and Tammy slowly got immersed again into affairs at Wamanta. As much as she hated to admit it, she missed Rick Hatton's autocratic presence and life appeared somewhat tedious. When she had finished in the office, she would wander round the farm. Mr Hampton had more work on his hands without Gerry around, but was always helpful in supplying Tammy with information. She learnt about the orchards she had seen in the distance, where apples, cherries, pears, plums, peaches and apricots grew in profusion. She also heard of a vineyard that was quite close by. He would take her on a tour of the district, he promised when things had settled down again.

His mention of tours reminded Tammy of something that had puzzled her during her day out with Rick Hatton, and she asked why she had not seen the sheep. Mr Hampton told her they were much farther up where it was cooler, so her earlier surmises that they were probably up in the hills had been correct. She thought of the distances. How much land, for goodness' sake, did Rick Hatton own? Mr Hampton grinned when this question was put to him. 'Don't rightly know,' he said. 'Give or take a few thousand acres, it'd be somewhere in the region of eighty thousand, I guess.'

Tammy sat stunned. To an English girl that sounded an awful lot of land. She would have to go a long way to get off Rick's territory. No wonder he was considered the big white chief, as Paula put it.

Friday afternoon brought Paula back from college, highly delighted to find Tammy once more back in residence. She was full of the coming dance. 'Gosh, Tammy, you must come. Everything's laid on, and the eats are fab. No one, but no one, misses the end of shearing dance. Mary's sister is making my dress. That reminds me, I must see if it's finished,' and she rushed towards the kitchen.

Putting the cover on the typewriter, Tammy sat deep in thought. She did not want to go to that wretched dance. On the other hand, she did not want to antagonise Rick Hatton again. It would only bring her to his notice once more. It would, she thought wistfully, be wonderful to see him again, even dancing with Diana. It was such a big occasion, according to Paula, that Miss Scott would be bound to attend.

Paula rushed back in. 'It's finished,' she cried. 'Mary's bringing it in tomorrow.' She whirled round, 'You wait until you see it, Tammy, Esmeralda's pretty clever with a needle. What are you wearing?' she demanded.

Tammy looked bewildered. 'Long or short dresses?' she asked.

Paula laughed. 'Long dresses, of course,' she replied. 'The men all dress up, too. It's an occasion.'

'I have one dress,' said Tammy. 'I don't know whether it's suitable or too dressy.'

'Couldn't possibly be too dressy. Come on, where is it, let me see it.' Paula caught hold of Tammy's hand and dragged her towards her room.

Paula gasped when she saw the dress, and fingered the gossamer gauze. 'It's beautiful, Tammy,' she said. 'It's kinda going to make mine look like this year's homespun,' she added wistfully.

'Shall I wear an ordinary dress, then?' asked Tammy anxiously. 'I'd hate to look overdressed.'

'Overdressed in that!' shrieked Paula. 'My, that will make Miss Diana Scott sit up. You wear it, Tammy, do you hear? About time the high and mighty Miss Scott had some competition.' She giggled. 'You sit next to me, Tammy, I'll take the overflow, they'll be queueing!'

'That,' said Tammy, looking slightly alarmed, 'settles it. Now let's see what else we have.' She started to search her wardrobe.

'Don't you dare,' said Paula. 'I'll never speak to you again if you don't wear that dress. What's the matter with you? If I'd your looks I'd be engaged by now. You got something against the opposite sex?' she demanded.

Tammy laughed. 'Oh Paula, there are other things in life, you know. I guess I haven't met the right one yet, that's all.' Her heart told her she had, but it was no use thinking that way; the sooner she realised that there was no hope for her, the happier she would be.

Mr Hampton proudly offered an arm to each young lady as they set off the following evening. Paula's blue satin dress was anything but homespun and suited her fair colouring. She had let her hair down and it fell to her shoulders. Tammy had tried to effect a severe style on hers, pulling it back and pinning it high at the back. Several wispy strands had already escaped and lay curling about her nape, adding to her look of fragility. Paula had taken one look at her and murmured roguishly, 'Poor Gerry!'

The hall was crowded when they arrived. Tammy breathed a sigh of relief. She would not look over-dressed. Everybody, it seemed, was in their glad rags. The woman all wore evening dresses, and a galaxy of colour met Tammy's wondering eyes. As Paula had mentioned earlier, there were not many occasions on which they could dress up, but this was one, and they all took advantage of it. The men were no less resplendent than the women. The majority wore dark suits, the more prominent members of the community were in tuxedos.

They were just settling down in their seats at the end of the hall when Tammy caught sight of Rick Hatton's tall figure. He wore a tuxedo, and Tammy's heart turned over. No wonder the girls fell for him! Bronzed and fair, he put the rest in the shade. There was something about him that put him head and shoulders above his companions. For one fleeting moment their eyes met. His were cold, there was no welcome in them. Tammy dropped hers instantly. She felt as if he had slapped her. She did not look that way again.

The opening dance struck up, and Tammy as well as the rest of the room watched Rick Hatton lead Diana Scott on to the floor. Diana was resplendent in black velvet, which clung to her figure. Tammy felt a stab of jealousy, and instantly quelled it; she hadn't Diana's curves, but at least she had more friends than Diana had. Miss Scott, it appeared, had a habit of antagonising all and sundry. Except, she sighed, Rick Hatton. But then she had no more time for gloomy thoughts. Paula had been perfectly right —within minutes Tammy was surrounded and the next five dances booked in a row.

Halfway through the evening she was grateful for

the remission period when refreshments were served. She had no less than three determined young men around her, all anxious to get her food. In the end she sent them all off on separate searches, one for sandwiches, one for cakes, and one for tea. Paula, having a healthy appetite, had gone to inspect the loaded tables and choose her portions. Mr Hampton had gone to join the men at the provisional bar at the other end of the room. Tammy sat back and took a breather. She had not been allowed to sit one dance out, and the rest of the evening promised to be just as hectic. She was searching in her bag for a stick of cologne when he spoke to her.

'Don't let it go to your head, will you, Delilah?'

Tammy glanced up quickly to meet the cold eyes of Rick Hatton. 'You go home with Mr Hampton. Is that understood?' he said grimly.

Her eyes flashed her answer. He nodded and outstared her. His eyes said, 'Try me.' Tammy looked down at her hands. Without another word, he moved on.

He couldn't, Tammy thought bitterly, let her enjoy one evening. He had spoilt it by just a few words. Although she was kept fully occupied for the rest of the evening, she longed for the end. It was positively the last dance she would attend. Rick Hatton would be given no more chances to get at her.

At last it was over. Thankfully Tammy said goodnight to her numerous admirers, and turned down the many offers to run her home. Paula had received permission from her father to be taken home by a neighbour's son, and judging by her flushed complexion was well satisfied by the evening's outcome. Rick Hatton, she noticed as she left with Mr Hampton, was standing in the hall's foyer engaged in conversation with a small clutch of people, Diana clutching his arm. Tammy did not look his way after that first glance, but knew he was watching her exit. She shrugged, wishing she had the courage to defy him and leave with at least three of her admirers.

Asking how she had enjoyed the evening, Mr Hampton settled her in the car. She had been the most sought after young lady, he said, and hadn't he said she would be? The car spluttered, then died out. He tried again, the same thing happened. He frowned and got out and opened the bonnet, then came back and searched for a torch in the glove compartment. 'Flooding again,' he growled. 'Dang me, they said they'd fixed it.' He scratched his head. 'Have to call them out, Tammy,' he said. 'You hold on, I'll see if I can get anyone going our way to drop you back. Might be some time before they arrive. I've just seen Jess Parker leave, now I'll have to wait till he gets back home. He'll have to collect his tools anyway.' He walked towards the hall.

Tammy heard a tap on the window and glanced out. One of the young men she had danced with stood there. 'In trouble?' he asked.

When Tammy explained, he offered, 'I can easily drop you off.'

Tammy called after Mr Hampton, who was about to disappear through the hall door. 'I've got a lift, Mr Hampton, shall I go on?'

'Okay, Tammy,' he shouted back. 'Tell Paula what's going on, will you? I might be some time.'

Tammy nodded. The young man, who she seemed to remember was called Don, drew his car up beside her, and she got in.

As they moved off, she smiled, 'It's Don, isn't it? I'm very grateful, thank you.'

'Don't mention it,' he grinned. 'I'm hoping you'll show a little more appreciation later on.'

Tammy stiffened. 'Now look here, let's get this straight, shall we? You offered me a lift, I accepted it. No offence meant, but that is all there is to it.'

'Relax, baby,' he drawled. 'Old man Hampton's going to be out some time—I ought to know, I fixed it.'

Tammy stared at him. 'You what!' she exclaimed.

She could sense him grin. 'You heard. I kinda thought when you turned all those offers down you'd be travelling back with him. You're the English girl Rick Hatton had up at his place, aren't you? Now I know I mightn't be quite so good-looking as his lordship, or have his cash, but I can give you a good time for all that.'

Tammy gasped; she suspected he was half drunk. For goodness' sake, he couldn't be much more than twenty, she thought. 'I'm afraid you're wasting your time,' she said coldly, and peered out of the window trying to see where they were. Not knowing the district, she was unable to pinpoint their position. 'Do you know where Wamanta is?' she demanded.

'Of course I do,' he replied jauntily. 'We're taking a roundabout route, there's plenty of time.'

Tammy got mad. 'Then stop the car, I'll walk it,' she said scathingly.

To her surprise he did. Tammy started to open the car door, but he stretched a long arm in front of her. 'I believe you're playing hard to get, but I'm game,' he slurred, and placed his other arm at the back of her and pulled her towards him.

Tammy had not enough strength to withstand his crippling hold on her and found herself propelled towards him. His lips searched her face and eventually found hers. She could smell the beer on his breath and struggled to free herself. His lips were warm and very moist, making Tammy feel like retching. She deliberately let herself relax, hoping he would loosen his hold on her. He did, murmuring, 'Been wanting to do that all night. Baby, you sure are lovely.'

She drew back slowly away from him, and he caressed her bare shoulder under her wrap. By now Tammy was through humouring him. She brought her arm up and gave him a stinging slap across his face. Don shook his head and stared at her, then grunted, 'Okay, let's play it rough,' and grabbed at her, missing her arm and catching the top of her dress. There was a tearing sound, and Tammy felt the strap snap away from her shoulder. She gasped.

The sound of the material tearing seemed to sober him, and he passed a hand over his forehead. 'Oh, hell, I guess I've really done it now.'

'Take me back to Wamanta,' said Tammy icily. 'At once, do you hear? You've ruined my dress!'

Don needed no second bidding and started the car up immediately. He started to apologise, explained that he had overdone the drink. He would willingly pay for the dress he said. He was still apologising when they eventually drew up at Wamanta some time later. Tammy got out thankfully, gave him a short lecture and wearily made her way into the homestead. She was more shaken than she had realised. Her legs felt like jelly. Her wrap had swung off her and she dragged it along with her.

'And where the devil have you been?'

Tammy blinked and raised her head slowly. She didn't have to look at Rick, she knew the voice by now. What was he doing here?

His eyes took in her appearance, staying on her shoulder. Tammy looked as well. Her left shoulder was completely bare, exposing the frilly edge of her strapless bra. She gasped and hastily pulled the torn material up, partially covering it.

His eyes were slits of ice. 'It's a little late for that, isn't it? What did you do to the poor devil—send him berserk?' His hand caught her wrist in a grip that hurt. 'Who was it?' he grated out.

Tammy felt she had really had enough. 'How do I know?' she said wearily. 'Apart from Don, it didn't occur to me to ask for credentials—besides,' she added slowly, 'he didn't mean to tear my dress, it was an accident.'

His lips curled. 'Was it really?' he said in a voice that said he didn't believe a word of it. 'He received no encouragement, of course, but you're forgetting I've seen how adept you can be in that line.'

She shook her head, and the tears gathered. What was the use?

'Tears now, I see,' he goaded. 'Well, that won't work either. Any more little tricks up your sleeve?'

Tammy wished she could hit him, but there was something about him that frightened her. She took a deep breath and said quietly, 'Why can't you leave me alone?'

A white line appeared around his mouth. Tammy held her breath. 'I thought you'd learnt your lesson,' he said softly, strengthening his hold on her wrist. She waited for the familiar jerk, but he dropped his hand from her, and turned away suddenly. She saw his fists clench. 'Get out of my sight,' he said in a low harsh voice.

Tammy fled.

CHAPTER TWELVE

MR HAMPTON did not get back until the early hours. Tammy, still awake, heard him arrive. Later she heard another car start up and drive off. Had Rick Hatton waited on for Mr Hampton? she wondered. She swallowed, trying to push the lump that rose in her throat each time the memory of the way he had looked at her rose before her eyes. He might call her 'Delilah', but his eyes had shouted 'Jezebel'. She buried her head in the pillow. Why couldn't he let her be? The tears escaped into the pillow. To think she had longed to see him! Better if she never ever saw him again. The very sight of her seemed to rile him. She recalled him dancing with Diana and the way he bent his head to catch something she was saying, once or twice she actually saw him smile. He had only to glance her way and the warmth in his eyes would die out as if quenched by ice. On these thoughts Tammy fell into a sleep of exhaustion.

Esme's singing woke her the following morning. She lay for a moment or two, then looked at her watch, gave a sharp exclamation on seeing it was past eight, and was almost out of bed before realising it was Sunday and sank back again. The hours were easy on Sunday. Breakfast was there if you wanted it. Paula rarely bothered. It was the one day she could lie in and she took full advantage of it.

There was a tap on the door and Mary poked her head round it. 'You want tea, Miss Tammy?' she said in her sing-song voice, accompanied by the usual wide grin.

Tammy smiled back and nodded. As she took the tea from Mary she mentioned, 'I'm not taking breakfast this morning, will you tell Esme, Mary?'

Mary nodded and beamed again. 'Esme say, how you grow big strong girl, huh?' She stood with arms akimbo, giving a fair imitation of a pose of Esme's. 'Mebbe you not want to grow big strong girl, huh?' She burst into peals of laughter. 'You okay, small girl, like me, huh?' Her laughter was infectious and Tammy couldn't help joining in.

After drinking her tea, Tammy got out of bed and wandered out to the shower. There was still no sign of Paula. It did occur to Tammy that she might have heard Rick Hatton's furious tirade last night and was giving her a wide berth to spare her feelings. She smiled mistily, it was just the sort of thing Paula would do, she really was a sweet girl.

She was dressing when she heard Paula call out to her. 'Tammy, I'm off to tennis. See you later. Picnic this afternoon, Rick's place. 'Bye!'

In the act of buttoning up a cool cotton frock, Tammy's fingers stilled. Oh, no, she wasn't meeting him again, not after last night. Wild horses would not drag her to Wamoshanta and neither would Rick

Hatton! How could Paula expect her to go? She sat down. Paula didn't know about last night. She couldn't. Both their rooms were well away from the hall. Tammy sighed. That was a blessing. Perhaps Mr Hampton did not know either? Then she remembered the car starting up later and the knowledge that Rick Hatton must have waited for him to come back. What had he told him? She closed her eyes. What if Mr Hampton should also turn against her? 'He wouldn't believe it,' she said aloud. If Mr Hampton asked what had happened, she would tell him. Rick Hatton had damned her without giving her a chance to explain, even though she had tried. She finished dressing and made her way down to the living room. For a moment she thought she was alone, then she heard a dry cough coming from the verandah and knew Mr Hampton was there, so she went out to him.

He was taking coffee and invited her to join him. Tammy poured herself a cup and sat down beside him. She heard him clear his throat once or twice, and knew he wanted to say something but didn't know how to start.

'About last night, Tammy,' he began, then noting Tammy's stiffened features, said hastily, 'Look, girl, I know Rick bawled you out, and I feel it's partly my fault. I should have made certain you were okay. I was too busy thinking of getting the car seen to. It's me Rick should have gone for. Not that I got away scot free, mind you. I got the length of his tongue, that's for sure.' He shook his head. 'Don't know what's got into him these days, he's like a bear with a sore head.' He gave Tammy a troubled look. 'Did he give you a bad time, Tammy?' he asked.

Tammy was at least thankful that Rick Hatton had not mentioned her state of disarray. 'No more than usual,' she replied quietly. 'I shouldn't have gone, you know, my just being around seems to upset him.'

Mr Hampton clenched his hands. 'Damned young fool,' he said once again. 'Can't expect you to shut yourself away.' He stared at the coffee pot. 'I thought he'd got over all that,' he said sorrowfully. 'Seems it was just wishful thinking.'

Tammy said nothing. She could have told Mr Hampton 'getting over it' was something Rick Hatton would never do. Then she remembered the picnic. 'Mr Hampton, I am not going to that picnic,' she said determinedly.

He sighed. 'No, I guess Rick realised that. He said you'd be excused.'

Tammy hurriedly concentrated on her coffee. It was Rick's way of telling her to keep out of his sight. Well, it suited her. Perhaps at last they had reached some agreement—to keep out of one another's sight. If only it lasted long enough, she might be able to fade out of the picture and make a run for home.

Paula helped dispel the gloom at lunch that day. Her chatter was always lively, she gave a hilarious account of her prowess at tennis. Her racquet, she said, appeared to have strings until she tried to hit something with it, then htey seemed to disappear. She only once mentioned the picnic and demanded to know why Tammy wasn't attending. Her father frowned at her and told her brusquely to, 'Leave it'. Paula looked somewhat surprised, but obeyed him and changed the subject. Tammy thought she would make a fine wife for a diplomat.

'We were one short,' continued Paula. 'There should have been eight of us, but one of the Eversley brothers was bunged up north to his aunt, went early this morning, he's not too keen on the aunt either, but he didn't mention going last night at the dance,' Paula mused.

Tammy kept her eyes on her plate. Rick Hatton had been very busy, she thought. It couldn't be coincidence. How had he found out? And why bother when he was so sure she had asked for trouble? He had called him a 'poor devil', hadn't he? Well, why punish him? She gave it up. It was all beyond her.

Paula did not like leaving Tammy behind when it was time to attend the picnic. Tammy knew it was only kindness that made her offer to stay and keep her company. Paula loved picnics and Tammy was determined she was not going to miss out on it. 'Honestly, Paula, I'm behind again with my mail. This is the only chance I get to catch up, so be a dear and let me get on with it.'

Tammy did write letters, only two, it was true, both to old school friends she had promised to keep in touch with. Her conscience smote her when she thought about Jonathan. If only she could rely on him to keep away she would send her address. Mr Bolton could not have seen him since, or had not mentioned the fact that he had met her; if he had, Tammy was sure Jonathan would have found some excuse to pay her a flying visit. She was in enough trouble without him complicating things. With any luck Rick Hatton would lose all interest; there were definite signs of it now, his latest attitude proved it.

She had gone to bed when they returned. Paula sought her out, full of righteous indignation. 'He's gone plain barmy!' she exclaimed, throwing herself in the cane chair in Tammy's room. 'And you should have seen Diana Scott prancing about like the cat's whiskers. She thinks she's as good as first lady. Honestly, Tammy, I thought Rick was pretty well on to her. If he does marry her, I'll ... I'll never speak to him again!'

Tammy's heart went cold. She tried to appear calm, and sat up in bed and looked at Paula.

'Now what's happened?' she asked, hoping she sounded nonchalant.

'Rick,' Paula answered impatiently, 'and that high and mighty Miss Scott. He's escorting her to Sydney next week for a visit to her relations.'

Tammy's eyebrows raised. Her heart beat a strong tattoo. 'Well, what's so awful about that?'

Paula looked at her, then sighed. 'I keep forgetting you're English,' she said, then sighed again. 'Well, when a man does that sort of thing in these parts it's almost the same as getting engaged. He trots off, as it were, to meet the rest of the relations, she's tried hard enough to get him. Course,' she brightened up, 'if he doesn't care much for the family, he just doesn't pop the question.' She looked at Tammy. 'If they all think as much of themselves as Diana Scott does, I can't see him going through with it. Rick's no snob.'

'It's the girl that counts, Paula,' said Tammy quietly. 'The relations shouldn't enter into it.'

Paula was examining her sandalled foot. 'I guess so,' she said, then frowned. 'I didn't hear Rick saying anything about the visits.' She looked up at Tammy. 'Perhaps she's made it up. I wouldn't put it past her. She's mad keen on Rick, not to mention his lolly.' She got up suddenly. 'Well, guess I'd better let you get your beauty sleep. Good thing I'm at college,' she said darkly. 'Seeing her strut around the town would give me the heeby-jeebies.' She walked out with hunched shoulders.

Tammy did not get much beauty sleep—Paula's news had seen to that. She knew she ought to feel relieved, as an engaged man Rick couldn't very well continue to pursue her. Miss Scott would very soon have something to say about that. In fact, she would hand Tammy her return ticket to England personally. Remembering the antagonistic look in her green eyes Tammy knew she would also personally escort her to the plane.

Paula returned to college next day and Tammy

tried to settle down to routine. Her heart felt enclosed in a steel band. Soon she would get used to the idea of Rick Hatton married and out of her life for good and all. She had to. No matter where they would have met, the result would have been the same, because of something that had happened in the past. Her eyes filled with tears. Why hadn't she made her heart behave? Deep down she had known she hadn't a chance. What cruel stroke of fate had brought them together in the first place? She jammed a sheet of paper in the typewriter and tried to concentrate on her work.

With Paula back at college, Tammy had hoped that would be the end of listening to Rick Hatton's affairs; exciting as they were to the locals, she didn't want to know. When Mr Hampton took up the subject later that evening on the verandah, Tammy could have screamed.

He was just as gloomy about it as Paula had been.

'Said he wasn't himself, didn't I, Tammy?' he muttered. 'Escorting her down to Sydney. Never done anything like it afore. Rick's no tame dog. He does the shouting, others do the jumping.' He shook his head. 'Sure sounds like wedding bells to me. They left this morning.'

Tammy could stand it no longer. 'Do you mind if I take a stroll in the garden, Mr Hampton?' she asked. 'It's such a lovely evening.'

He nodded, then grinned. 'If I was twenty years younger, Tammy, I'd come with you.'

The sweet-scented garden enfolded Tammy as she walked slowly through it. Her heart was heavy. It could all have been so different. There had been so much she had wanted to see, yet now, no matter what beauty her eyes alighted on, it would have a bittersweet echo. Perhaps in time all that had happened would return only as a dream, a dream of what might have been. She thought of Rick Hatton and Diana against her will. Try as she might to shut them out, they kept intruding. Would she have to watch them marry? No! She couldn't. She must leave. Somehow she must find a way. There wouldn't be a better opportunity. Sydney was miles away.

She was so immersed in working out ways and means of escape that she did not hear the authoritative 'Tammy?' It was repeated, and this time she did look up and stared at the man standing before her. She still couldn't grasp the fact that he was actually there. 'Jonathan?' she said. The next moment she was caught, held in a tight grip, and being kissed in no uncertain manner.

'You deserve a spanking,' said Jonathan severely. 'Why didn't you let me know your address?'

When Tammy got her berath back she tried to disentangle herself from his arms, but he held her tighter. 'Because you cheated,' she said. 'I saw Todd on the plane, trying very hard to make himself invisible.'

Jonathan laughed. 'Well, my pet, I was worried about you. He got a rocket when he lost you.' He held her away from him and studied her closely. 'You've got a slight tan, suits you.'

'You can't possibly see in this light,' said Tammy indignantly. 'What are you doing here, anyway?'

'I didn't want you to forget me,' he said on a bantering note. 'You see, I thought if I kept on popping up, you just might decide you can't live without me.' He pulled her close to him. 'I have missed you, poppet,' he said softly.

'Oh, Jonathan!' wailed Tammy. It was all she could do not to burst into tears.

Jonathan took this as a healthy sign. 'And you have missed me?' he demanded.

Tammy nodded, it was true she had missed him. She had missed his kindness, his thoughtfulness and his devotion.

'Good. Then we'll marry,' he said brightly.

'No!' wailed Tammy. 'Oh, Jonathan, I just don't know. I only know I want to go home—tomorrow or the next day, as soon as possible.' She burst into tears and wept into his jacket lapels.

Jonathan let her have her cry, then carefully wiped the tears away with his handkerchief.

'Can it wait until Wednesday, poppet?' he asked anxiously. 'I've fixed an appointment to have a look at one of the vineyards, Bolton told me the wines are good.'

Tammy sniffed, and nodded. 'As long as it's this week, it doesn't matter.' She swallowed. 'Jonathan, did you say Mr Bolton?'

Jonathan nodded. 'He also got a rocket,' he said grimly. 'Never thought to mention he'd met you all those weeks ago.'

'Have you met Mr Hampton?' queried Tammy.

Jonathan placed an arm round her waist as they started to walk back to the house. 'Yes, he sent me to find you. Said something about my being his substitute, whatever that means.'

Tammy gave a watery chuckle. 'He said if he was twenty years younger he'd accompany me on my walk.'

'Oh, did he?' murmured Jonathan. 'I see I shall have to keep an eye on Mr Hampton.'

It wasn't Mr Hampton who wanted watching where she was concerned, but Tammy thought it wise to hold her peace. Jonathan was a mild enough man normally; if he had an inkling of how she had been treated by one certain person he would attempt to knock that person's block off. She thanked providence that he had turned up when Rick Hatton was miles away.

Another thought struck her. She would be putting Mr Hampton in an awkward fix if she informed him of her decision to go home. Well, she wouldn't tell him. She would leave him a note thanking him for his kindness; he would know very well why she had gone, but at least he could show the note to Rick Hatton afterwards to prove he had no idea of her plans. That way Rick Hatton could not take it out on him.

'Jonathan, don't mention the fact that we're leaving to Mr Hampton. It's a bit awkward, he's not the boss, you see, and he might feel he ought to get permission for me to leave, and that could take weeks. I'm so homesick I couldn't bear to have to wait that long.'

Jonathan did not probe. He guessed there was more to it than that. He knew Tammy was unhappy and wanted to go home, and that was good enough for him. 'Right, poppet,' he said calmly.

Just before they entered the house Tammy turned to him. 'Where are you staying?' she asked, feeling guilty at not even remembering to ask him how long he had been travelling. He might be dead on his feet for all she knew.

'The Queen's,' he answered. 'Not bad for a town that size,' then he pulled Tammy closer. 'Still, it won't be for long, will it, pet? I've got what I came for.'

Mr Hampton materialised out of the shadows on the verandah. Tammy was sure he had heard Jonathan's last remark. She just hoped he didn't do any adding up.

After coffee and something a bit stronger for the men, Jonathan left for the town and a comfortable bed at the Queen's, arranging to pick Tammy up the following morning and take her with him on the visit to the vineyard. Mr Hampton okayed these arrangements. He felt it was time Tammy began to enjoy herself. He teased her a little before she escaped to bed.

'A fine man, Tammy.' He gave her a twinkling look. 'Not the only wedding on the agenda, eh? He's got his eye on you, my girl, and I'd say,' he looked down at the drink in hand, 'I'd say he was a very determined man. He might act kinda casual, but he's got a head on his shoulders, yes, sir.'

As Tammy prepared for bed she thought of Mr Hampton's words. Mr Hampton was nobody's fool. He'd taped Jonathan for a start. Only Tammy knew how determined Jonathan could be. That casual air of his had fooled many a business rival to their eventual cost.

That night she dreamt of being pursued by a man on a white horse; as the hoofbeats came nearer she recognised the man as Rick Hatton, and he was waving a piece of white paper at her. Tammy ran faster.

CHAPTER THIRTEEN

THE sun awoke her the next morning. She lay for a moment or two, watching the pattern of the sunbeams playing on the ceiling. She wondered what it was like in England. Remembering the icy winds and the foggy nights, she shivered. The coldness she felt deep inside her could not be put down to the weather, it encased her heart. She jumped out of bed hastily; thoughts like that were usless. Somehow she had to get through today, tomorrow she would be on her way home. Tomorrow . . . picking up her toilet bag and towel, she made her way to the shower; she would not think about tomorrow. Time enough for that in the long miserable days to come.

They had just finished breakfast when Jonathan arrived. He wore a cream-coloured suit, his dark crisp hair gleaming in the morning light. Tammy went to meet him and was caught in his arms before she could wish him good morning. Mr Hampton watched indulgently and grinned.

'Ready, darling?' asked Jonathan.

Tammy nodded, then picked up her light jacket, collected her bag and turned to Mr Hampton. 'See you later Mr Hampton, and thank you for giving me time off.'

He nodded. 'You enjoy yourself, girl.'

With Jonathan's arm around Tammy, they walked out to the car. Tammy felt a stab of conscience. She would say the same tomorrow, but there would be no 'later'. She had more or less worked out how to get her cases out of the homestead without Mr Hampton seeing. He always did the rounds of the farm between seven and nine, returning for breakfast later. She would get Jonathan to arrive between those hours. After he had read the note she would leave him, he would understand. She bit her lip; it would have to be a carefully worded note. She mentally thought it out as the car swept out of the homestead grounds.

Jonathan, glancing at her lost in concentration, remarked, 'What's up, poppet? You look worried.'

Tammy blinked quickly, then smiled at him. 'I'll just be relieved when we're home,' she said truthfully.

Frowning, Jonathan asked, 'Has it been as bad as all that?'

Tammy started. That was stupid of her. She had forgotten how perceptive Jonathan could be where she was concerned. 'Of course not,' she replied hastily. 'It's been a marvellous experience, but I've been terribly homesick. I guess I'm just a home girl after all.'

He grinned and caught her hand lying in her lap; he squeezed it. 'This time tomorrow,' he promised, 'we'll be on the way.'

Tammy looked away, carefully studying the passing landscape. Fields of wheat bending slightly in the breeze looked like golden carpets in the sun. This was the outer edge of the farm. After a momentary glance, Tammy did not see the wheat, she saw a furious six-footer with blazing eyes looking at her as if she was something that had just crawled out from under a stone. And that, she thought dully, was her last sight of him. Fitting really, it had begun the same way, on that very first day. She gave herself a mental shake and turned her attention to Jonathan, asking him to fill her in on the latest happenings at home.

The sun was well up by the time they reached the vineyard. Tammy had her straw hat, Jonathan collected his panama from the back seat and putting it on, held an assisting hand out to Tammy as she got out of the car. Then placing a possessive arm around her, he led her towards a group of buildings on the edge of the vineyard. The door of a shed-like building opened as they walked towards it and a man came towards them. His gaily patterned shirt struck a cheerful note against the grey drab of the buildings behind him. He was tanned almost black. On the back of his head perched an old straw hat that had seen many summers. His welcoming hand was held out long before he reached them.

'Day, Mr Drew,' he grinned. 'Jim Daly.' he gestured towards the building he had just left. 'Got some tea on the go, or would you like to take a look around first?'

Jonathan looked down at Tammy. 'Drink, pet?' he asked.

Tammy shook her head. 'I'm not really thirsty yet, but I'll have one if you want one.'

Jonathan shook his head. 'We'll sample something cooler after the look round, shall we, Mr Daly?'

Mr Daly grinned. 'Got some really fine wines I'm hoping you'll sample,' he said. 'This way, Miss... er...'

'Dainton,' supplied Jonathan. 'Lead the way, Mr Daly.'

Tammy had only seen vineyards at a distance during the ride up from Adelaide. The first thing that struck her was the orderliness of row upon row of staked vines. The leaves were light green and nestling in amongst the foliage clustered bunches of grapes. As they passed the rows, Mr Daly would murmur, 'Table', or 'Wine'. A much smaller grape was designated 'Dried'. Gorgeous large black grapes with skins that shone, and pale green luminescent clusters, made Tammy forget her troubles in the wonder of it all.

They did not inspect the whole vineyard, as it ran into acres. Jonathan professed himself satisfied with what he had seen, then pushed his panama to the back of his head and suggested that Mr Daly carry on with the rest of the programme. Tammy had been looking at the clusters of grapes to be used for wine. It seemed a pity, she thought, that they were going to be crushed into pulp. Jonathan brought her out of her musings by placing an arm about her shoulders and pulling her close.

'Come on, darling, we shall now sample the end product,' he grinned.

Tammy was swung around and found herself looking straight into the cool grey eyes of Rick Hatton. She stared. It couldn't be! He was in Sydney. But that tall figure that seemed to fill the whole path between the vines was real enough.

Mr Daly's surprised, 'Why, hallo, Rick. Thought you was in Sydney,' proved to Tammy she was not having hallucinations.

'Day, Jim,' was the drawled reply. 'Got back this morning.' Although he spoke to Mr Daly his eyes were on Jonathan. Jonathan's arm was still holding her close and Tammy felt glad of the protection, as she moved closer to Jonathan. She saw Rick Hatton's eyes narrow at the slight move. 'Good morning, Miss Dainton,' he said softly. 'Taking a day off?'

Tammy started, then pulled herself together. Rick Hatton's reign of terror was over. Jonathan was here, wasn't he?

'Mr Hampton gave his permission,' she said quietly. She then turned to Jonathan. 'Jonathan, this is my boss, Mr Hatton,' she ended lamely, then suddenly recalling she hadn't finished the introductions added hastily, 'Mr Hatton, this is Mr Drew, a close friend.'

Jonathan laughed at that. 'Very close,' he grinned, holding his hand out to Rick Hatton. 'How do you do.'

For one awful moment it looked as if Rick Hatton would ignore the outstretched hand, then he held his hand out, and the men shook hands. In karate they bow before they start combat, thought Tammy, here they shake hands. It wouldn't take long for Jonathan to size up Rick Hatton's attitude towards her. Tomorrow couldn't come soon enough for Tammy.

'Going to give them some tasters, Rick,' explained Mr Daly. Tammy wondered why he should bother to explain his movements to Rick Hatton.

'Sure,' Rick drawled in reply. 'Interested in vineyards, Mr Drew?'

Jonathan looked faintly amused. He was almost a household name where wines were concerned. 'Couldn't make a living without them,' he grinned.

Mr Daly looked shocked. 'This, Rick, is the Jonathan Drew—Southern Wines Limited.'

Rick Hatton raised his eyebrows. He gave Tammy a calculating look and murmured, 'Well, well.'

Tammy knew what he was thinking and flushed slightly. He had even doubted Jonathan's existence, let alone his wealth. Even so, she was slightly puzzled. What would Rick Hatton know of Southern Wines? He was a grazier, wasn't he? A nasty suspicion entered her thoughts, and the following events did nothing to alleviate it.

They proceeded to the reception area. Rick Hatton showed no inclination to leave them and Tammy was furious. He drew Jonathan aside and Tammy had no option but to walk with Mr Daly. From the questions she could hear him asking Jonathan he was no stranger to the wine industry.

The entered a cool garden lounge and Jonathan saw Tammy settled in one of the cane chairs. To Tammy's disgust she watched Rick Hatton calmly settle himself in a chair beside her. Jonathan sat on her other side and Mr Daly went in search of the refreshments.

'So you've decided to give us a trial, have you?' Rick Hatton asked Jonathan.

Tammy started. She did not like the 'us' bit at all.

'Bolton said you had some promising wines,' explained Jonathan.

'So that's how you knew,' drawled Rick Hatton his eyes on Tammy.

He isn't referring to the wines, thought Tammy.

'Back to work tomorrow, Miss Dainton,' said Rick Hatton with a certain amount of determination in his voice.

Jonathan gave him a sharp look. Tammy held her breath; please don't give the game away, Jonathan, she prayed.

'I hope you've no objection to my borrowing her for a couple of days,' asked Jonathan, his blue eyes innocent.

'As long,' drawled Rick Hatton, 'as it is only a couple of days. I've some urgent work on hand; under the circumstances, however, it can wait a day or two.'

Tammy couldn't look at either man. She gazed at her hands clenched in her lap.

Mr Daly returned laden with a tray of bottles.

Glasses were produced and the serious business of tasting began.

'Try this one, Drew,' offered Rick Hatton, selecting a bottle of red wine and pouring a glass for Jonathan. 'It's considered unique for these parts.'

Jonathan sipped the wine, rolled it across his tongue for a second or so and raised his eyebrows, then nodded slowly and held his hand out for the bottle. Rick Hatton gave it to him and Jonathan studied the label. 'As you say, unique,' he said. He turned to Tammy. 'Try it, darling, see what you think.'

Taking it, she noticed Rick Hatton's eyes narrow at the endearment. Dutifully tasting it, she found it was a heady wine. She frowned, then looked at Jonathan. 'I'm not sure,' she said, 'but I think it's '68.'

Jonathan chuckled and pulled her towards him, kissing her quickly on the lips. 'Good for you, poppet!' He turned to Rick Hatton, who was beginning to look a little murderous. 'I taught her, you know.' He looked at Mr Daly. 'I think we can do a deal, Mr Daly.'

Mr Daly beamed. 'Like to come to the office, then, and we'll iron something out.'

Jonathan stood up. He held out his hand for Tammy, but Rick Hatton drawled, 'I'll keep Miss Dainton entertained during your absence.'

It was clear that Jonathan did not like that, but there was nothing he could do about it. He looked at Tammy. 'Don't you dare move,' he commanded, and followed Mr Daly out of the garden towards the buildings.

Tammy's heart beat erratically. She refused to look at Rick Hatton, her eyes were on the glass of red wine she still held. The glass was taken from her and placed on the table.

'So you would go that far, would you?' he said softly.

'I don't,' she answered quietly, wishing her heart would behave, 'know what you're talking about.'

'Oh, yes, you do. Look at me!'

Tammy found her eyes obeying that command against her will. She was lost in their grey depths.

'Is that what you want, Delilah? A tame lapdog for a husband?' he demanded.

'Jonathan is no tame lapdog!' she replied furiously.

'Where you're concerned he certainly is,' he ground out. 'He's so crazy over you he can't see straight.'

'That,' said Tammy through clenched teeth, 'makes a welcome change from some of the treatment I've received in this part of the world!'

'Okay,' he ground out harshly. 'What do you want me to do? Crawl to you? You know I'll never do that. If it's any consolation, he's not the only one who can't see straight. I've been that way ever since I first set eyes on you.'

Tammy couldn't believe her ears. Her wide eyes opened wider still. He was telling her he loved her! She shook her head bewilderingly. 'It's not true ... I don't ...' She glared at him. 'You're just making it up. It's just another way of getting at me.' She swallowed. 'Well, you're wasting your time. I'm not falling for that . . . that fairy story!'

He gripped her hand hard. 'You'd better believe it,' he drawled, 'or you're in for a few shocks before you're much older. I'm courting you, Delilah, and when I say courting, I mean courting. It's an old-fashioned word that has an old-fashioned ending, and I intend to get that old-fashioned ending. Do you understand?'

Tammy closed her eyes. Surely even Rick Hatton wouldn't go that far? She wished she could believe what he had told her. Her heart wanted so much to believe. If she hadn't known about his stepmother, if he hadn't treated her as he had, she might have been able to believe. The hand that still held hers was strong, and she longed to place it against her cheek, to tell him how much she loved him. She felt the prick of tears. Why had he had to come back? Why couldn't she have been spared this last final attempt to hurt her?

Her face felt stiff. She shook her head slowly. 'I'm sorry,' she said in a voice so low he could only just catch it, 'it's no use.'

She heard him catch his breath and the hand holding hers tightened its grip. 'I'm not letting you go, Delilah. You're mine, I'm your man, and you know it. If it takes a lifetime I'll prove it to you,' he said firmly.

The sound of voices approaching helped Tammy to

recover partially. She snatched her hand away from Rick, and hastily stood up. She walked to meet Jonathan, wanting to get as far away as possible from the devastating nearness of Rick Hatton. As long as she could keep her distance she knew she was safe. If he took her in his arms she would be lost.

CHAPTER FOURTEEN

'ANYWHERE in particular you'd like to go, poppet?' queried Jonathan when they got back into the car after many handshakes from a delighted Mr Daly, and a watchful Rick Hatton.

Tammy shook her head. Anywhere as long as it was out of a certain person's sight, she thought. She did not look back as they left the vineyard; those purposeful grey eyes she knew followed them, as the car slowly gathered speed and left the vineyard behind.

Her head in a whirl, Tammy tried to concentrate on Jonathan's lighthearted comments. 'Who is this Rick Hatton character, anyway?' he asked suddenly.

Tammy roused herself to answer. 'Just about everybody around these parts,' she replied wearily. 'He owns most of the town too.'

'He's got a good thing going with that vineyard,' said Jonathan.

Tammy stared at him. 'Does he own that too?' she asked.

Jonathan nodded. 'I gather Mr Daly is being given pretty well free rein; he probably went through a bad spell and Hatton bought him out, it happens often enough in the business. It's Hatton's name on the offcial documents, though. I presume it's the same one, R. S. Hatton, is that right?'

Tammy nodded. She had seen Rick's bold signature often enough on letters. Can't we find another subject? she thought desperately.

They eventually settled to have lunch out, a ride touring the orchard district and dinner back at the Queen's. Tammy shut out all other thoughts. This was her last day in Australia, and Rick Hatton would not ruin the rest of the day for her. He had tried hard enough, but it had not come off.

It was late when Jonathan eventually took her back to Wamanta. She had warned him not to mention the following day's agenda when they got to the homestead; she had not forgotten the way Mr Hampton had materialised on the verandah, and nothing, but nothing must go wrong. Although she had tried very hard to appear gay during the evening, she couldn't banish Rick Hatton or his words from her thoughts. Her only hope lay in escape, and she had to take the one chance she was being given.

Jonathan's possessive kiss and hug before he saw her into the homestead did nothing to alleviate her misery, only added to it. As she walked slowly down the hall towards the night quarters, tears pricked her eyes. Then a voice that made her stiffen and halt in her tracks spoke close behind her.

'Did you enjoy the evening, Delilah?'

Tammy did not turn round. 'Thank you, yes,' she said. She had given up wondering how he seemed to be everywhere at once.

'Come into the study, I want to talk to you,' he ordered.

As usual, not will you, she thought crossly. 'It's late, can't it wait?' She had a vague recollection of saying that before. It hadn't worked then. It wasn't going to work now either, she thought wearily. She was right.

'Now you know better than that, don't you?' he said softly.

What, thought Tammy, did it matter? For the very last time Rick could manipulate the strings where she was concerned. She might as well humour him.

He closed the study door and stood in front of it, looking down at her. His gaze travelled slowly over her face. Tammy's eyes met his squarely. Memorise me, Mr Hatton, after tonight that's all you'll have left, went through her mind.

'Is it hate, Delilah? Or is it love?' he said softly.

Tammy's heart missed a beat. Careful, she warned it, this man's a professional in this line.

'You should know,' she said quietly. 'You're quite good at both, aren't you?'

He took a quick breath and she saw his hands clench.

'I'm trying to keep my distance, Delilah, but you're not making it easy, are you?' he drawled.

Tammy couldn't bear to look at him. She turned away and walked over to a chair near the desk, keeping her back to him, and stood with her hands gripping the chair.

'You've got to fight me every inch of the way, haven't you?' he demanded harshly. 'If you think I gave you a bad time, what do you think I went through? Why do you think I sent you back to Mr Hampton? To protect you, that's why. I couldn't trust myself any longer. Half the time I wanted to throttle you for what you were doing to me, the other half, I wanted to do what I want to do right now, kiss you into submission. I could, and you know it,' he said softly.

Tammy couldn't give in. She was no longer sure of herself or of him. 'What happened?' she asked in a low bitter voice. 'What decided things in my favour? Couldn't you bear to see your little plaything fade out of the picture? Would life become dull without me to taunt and hurt?'

There was silence for a second or two; when he did speak his voice was low, no longer vibrant and sure.

'Life would not only become dull, Delilah, it would become meaningless. I can't remember ever asking anyone's forgiveness, but I am asking for yours. You once said I was punishing you for what happened years ago, remember? I was not only punishing you but myself as well. I was a goner from the first flash of your pansy blue eyes. I knew very well I was going under fast, but how I fought it! Like father, like son, hammering in my brain. What happened to my father wasn't going to happen to me.' He moved closer to Tammy. Tammy felt his nearness, but couldn't move.

'Trouble is, Delilah, when you hurt someone you love, you suffer twice as much as they do. I wanted to believe you were a no-good gold-digger, someone on the make. Anything would have done so long as I could wipe you out of my system. I went on looking for something to pin on you and when I found what I was looking for the whole thing blew up in my face.'

Tammy's hands were gently lifted from the chair, she was pulled back against his lean hard body. Rick spoke into her hair.

'The night of the dance,' he continued softly, 'I knew you'd been offered a lift. I waited for you to return. When I saw the state you were in . . . I think I would have throttled you if I hadn't had the sense to keep my hands off you. There it was, Delilah, just what I'd been waiting for—proof of what I'd hoped you were. I ought to have been shouting for joy. It was over, I told myself. I was free.' He was silent so long that Tammy held her breath for a second or two, then he continued, 'I walked the night away, just kept on walking. I told myself I'd send you away. I knew you'd go fast enough if given the opportunity. Then it hit me good and hard—I couldn't do it! I didn't care what the hell you were, you could have been anything, but I loved you so much it didn't matter, nothing mattered. You were mine. I got the story out of young Eversley. I was so damn jealous I couldn't rest until I knew the whole of it. It was as well for him that he only tried to kiss you, or I would have killed him.'

Tammy's defences were crumbling fast. She managed to surface long enough to ask, 'But you went to Sydney with Diana to meet her relations?'

'I went to Sydney yes. I did meet a relation of hers, an uncle in fact, he's in the land estate business. Why?... Oh, I see,' an amused note crept into his voice. 'So folk did a little adding up, did they, and made two and two make five?' His arms tightened around her. 'Do you want to know what I really went for? There's an isolated ranch on the edge of my grazing land. It doesn't come in my property, so I bought it. It was abandoned years ago, drought beat them, but with the improved roads and bores, it could still become a thriving cattle station. I planned to do just that. I also planned,' he held her tighter, 'to take my Delilah up there. It would have been a rough and tough courtship, but you would have seen things my way in the end.'

Tammy closed her eyes. She thought of Jonathan and the proposed trip home.

He said it for her. 'Are you still leaving in the morning?' he asked softly.

Tammy started. She ought to have known better. It was his town, after all. Someone must have heard Jonathan make the plane reservations.

'I don't know,' she said, her voice trembling a little. If only he would move away from her, she could begin to think straight.

His arms tightened still more, and she felt her back would break. Then they fell away from her. She felt

188

lost without their warmth.

'I haven't given you much time, have I?' he said quietly. 'I know you're going early. If you decide it's Jonathan, well, that's that. I guess I've left things a bit late.' His voice was mild, it sounded somehow beaten—he, of all people! Her hands were clenched by her side.

'Go to bed, Delilah, perhaps you'll dream the answer,' he said gently, pushing her to the door.

Tammy needed no second bidding. The tears were cascading down her face as she dashed for the sanctuary of her room.

She fell asleep lulled by the turn of events. Her tired brain refused to assimilate the facts. Rick's quiet voice asserting his love washed gently over her, blotting out all else. The morrow would take care of itself . . . and Jonathan. A tiny frown creased her forehead.

The moment Tammy opened her eyes the next morning a feeling of exhilaration washed over her. Something wonderful had happened! She couldn't have dreamt it. Rick had said he loved her, had loved her all the time! She jumped out of bed, wanting to shout her happiness to the awakening world, but the thought of Jonathan suddenly halted her in her tracks, and she sat down heavily on the bed. He would be there in . . . she glanced at her watch . . . one hour's time. She frowned. Ought she to ring him? Slowly she shook her head. That was the coward's way out. She must tell him the truth. It wasn't going to be easy, and she must face him while she did so. She owed him that much. What if he decided on staying on for a while? How could she keep the two men from coming to blows? Once the decision was made Rick would assert his authority in no uncertain manner.

Tammy smiled mistily. He always would. It didn't matter, she wouldn't have him any other way. She showered and dressed, and while she brushed her hair she tried to think of a coherent explanation of her behaviour to give Jonathan. Her brush ceased its relentless strokes through her hair. How do you explain love? She grimaced at her reflection. One minute you loathed someone, the next . . . she gave it up.

Mary's tap told her she had only fifteen minutes to wait for Jonathan's arrival. As she drank her morning tea and the minutes ticked slowly away, her new-found confidence slowly deserted her. She would glance at her watch every five seconds or so. At five to eight she stood up, took a deep breath, ran a nervous hand through her hair and left the room.

She heard a car draw up outside the homestead, and with apprehensive eyes went to meet Jonathan.

Opening the screen door, she met the cool grey eyes of Rick Hatton.

'He's not coming, Delilah,' he said quietly.

Tammy stared at him.

'He's leaving on the same plane. You could see him off, but I'd rather you didn't.'

Tammy's first thought was that Jonathan mightn't be in a fit state to be seen. Her eyes showed her concern.

Rick acknowledged the look. 'He's okay. We kinda had a little talk earlier on,' he drawled.

Tammy still wasn't sure. 'Then why shouldn't I see him off?' she demanded.

'Because,' he said softly, 'I didn't spend the night outside your room making sure you didn't decide in his favour and leave earlier than intended to have you jump on that plane at the last minute. I'm taking no chances, Delilah.' He looked behind her, and she knew he was looking for the cases. When he was satisfied she hadn't packed, he grinned at her. 'So it was love, was it?' he said softly, and moved purposefully towards her.

Tammy was back to the mad stage with Rick. She glared at him. She had never had a choice. In his usual high-handed manner he'd taken over. Why, for all he knew she might have loved Jonathan!

'I can still make that plane,' she declared. 'And what's more, I'm packing!' she shouted, and rushed back into the homestead.

Rick caught her before she reached her room.

'Like I said, Delilah,' he murmured pulling her back into his arms, 'it's going to be a rough and tough courtship. I'm going for a submission, no holds barred.'

After she had been thoroughly kissed, he demanded, 'Are you going to see it my way?'

All Tammy could see were moons and stars. She was still a little mad at him, but when he eventually released her all she could say was, 'Rick Hatton, you need a shave!'

He grinned. 'Do I, my love? Well, I did warn you it was going to be rough, didn't I? It's been the longest night of my life,' he finished ruefully. He then picked her up in his arms and carried her out of the homestead and settled on a secluded seat in the scented garden.

'Rick,' she murmured a little while later, 'what did happen about Jonathan?'

He gave her a considering look before he answered. 'It appears, my love, that Jonathan knows you a little better than you gave him credit for, and for that,' he said darkly, 'I nearly did give him a punch on the nose. However, I managed to restrain myself. You know, Delilah, a man in love always recognises a rival. He'd guessed how it was between us, but he was willing to risk you accepting him on the rebound as it were, until I informed him that there wasn't going to be any rebound,' he finished grimly.

Tammy nestled closer.

'Shall we make it a happy ending this time?' He murmured, his lips following the curve of her throat. 'Will you, Delilah, take Richard Samson Hatton to your lawful wedded husband?'

Tammy's eyes opened wide and she pulled herself out of his arms to see his face. His grey eyes held a light that made her heart turn over. 'Richard Samson . . .' she said in wonderment.

He nodded slowly. 'Guess I knew all that time ago just how it was going to be.'